Written by:
Cheraee C.

DEVIANCY
I LOVE THE THRILL

MOCY PUBLISHING, LLC

Detroit, Michigan

DEVIANCY: I Love The Thrill

ISBN 978-1-94083-13-2-9

Published by Mocy Publishing, LLC.
Website: www.mocypublishing.com
Email: info@mocypublishing.com

Introduction: The Art of Deviancy

The bureaucracy of Oakland law was flooded with a bunch of snooty, tight-creased suit wearing capitalists who were sexually oppressive with fetishes dying to be eased, challenged, and released. They used their downtime to prey on inner city sexually deviant citizens whom they could exploit with their government salary. No matter what city, state, or country you went to there was always a sex scandal somewhere. The queen of sex scandals in the hood though was a top flight erotic mogul who went by the name of Infiniti Brooks.

Infiniti Brook's raw reputation was so viral that she had enough colorful subscribers to start her own minority. From owning her own chain of adult stores (Infiniti SX), adult entertainment safe house, and owning her own sex toy line, Infiniti had all types of billionaires in her back pocket, fifth pocket, purse pocket, corner pocket, all pockets. Her billionaires couldn't stop mentally churning the motions that she would whip on them.

Lingering inside Infiniti's Lathrup Village branch was a local news anchor from Channel 4 (Quad Lewinski.) Quad was always the first to test Infiniti's sex toys. Her latest invention was known as "Pinnacle" and its sole purpose was to tantalize the vagina with an array of temperature changes. Quad wired Infiniti 1500 bucks every time he paid her a visit when she dropped a new toy. All Infiniti had to do was do a personal demonstration for Quad as he sat back, loosened up his tie, let his dress pants drape on his ankles, fondled himself, and watched. Infiniti and Quad was making way to their usual dressing room after

Infiniti grabbed a Pinnacle off the shelf, but Quad stopped her dead in her tracks.

"Infiniti, have you checked your account?"

"No, I didn't. You ain't never played me on my monies before. Should I?"

"I put 3000 in your account today. I know we've had a mean streak and I ain't trying to break it, but today I want to watch a new gal play with herself. Is that cool?"

"That's cool with me; I gotta shoot some moves anyway. Let me go holler at my girl Navy. You can just wait in the room back there and I'll send her in. I'll give her the toy too. No need for my use."

"Cool."

Good, I didn't feel like playing with myself anyway. I'm a C.E.O. what I look like? Maybe Quad and I should negotiate another deal. I'll give him a new girl every time he comes to play, and I'll switch up the branches too long as he pays what he weighs. I still don't understand why he won't let me setup these personal sessions at a hotel or something, but that's another topic for another day. Hopefully Navy will get down with the get down.

"Aye Navy, I need you to do something for me."

"Sure, what you need?"

"I have a client in the room who wants you to test out Pinnacle for him. Is you cool with that or nah?"

"I don't recall seeing masturbation in the job description."

"You wanna lose your promotion and raise all in a minute or do you won't this fat $500 dollar tip?"

"I'm tripping, which room he in?"

"He's in the last room to the left. All you got to do is test the toy out on yourself. He's not going to touch or nothing. All he wants to do is watch you. I'll transfer the $500 into your account before I leave. I gotta make a run. I don't know if I'll be back today so you know what to do. Here take the toy," Infiniti handed Navy the unopened box.

"You're not sending me in there with a creep are you or to be raped because if you are you can take this job and your $500 tip and shove it up your anus with a dry, plastic dildo."

"I told you I have high paying clients who pay me money to make their fantasies come true. I can put you on or put you out because you're stalling and your insulting my intelligence."

"I'm sorry I just never did anything so random like this before."

"It's a first time for everything. Think about the $500 and how much more money you can make especially if he requests you. This was all at his request. Now gone in there and get it over with before you scare him away."

Going in the room and closing the sound proof door behind her, Navy was more nervous than a student on the first day of school. She saw Quad sitting across from her waiting for the show to begin. Navy closed her eyes and took a deep breath. She was just about to unbutton her skinny jeans when Quad broke her concentration.

"Your nametag says Navy is that how you pronunciate it?"

"Yeah you said it right."

"I rocks with Infiniti the long way, but I need a new deviant girl. Do you think you can handle that role?"

"I'm scoring roles and never once thought about acting or the big screen," Navy thought.

Quad went in his pockets and pulled out a wad of money. The wad held ten 100 dollar bills tightly.

"Here's 1000, watching is getting corny. That's what I paid Infiniti to do, but you I want you to test Pinnacle out on me. I'm Infiniti's product test dummy."

"Um, I don't think that's a good idea," Navy felt gauche.

"I'm not paying you to think or like my ideas."

"You are a male; you should use a male sex toy. Infiniti manufactured this toy for a female and the female anatomy. Unless you got a clitoris down there, this toy ain't for your alley."

"I do have a clitoris."

"How I thought you was a him? You mean to tell me you're really a shim? A she-he? A shemale?"

"Yeah I am now that you know let's get it cracking with Pinnacle. I got to hit the streets and follow up on some news leads."

"We ain't about to get nothing cracking. Only thing you need to crack is some Chap Stick for your dry, crusty lips. I feel like I just got catfished so here's what's about to happen. I'm going to keep your generous tip and forget this ever happened. We'll let Infiniti think what she thinks, and next time you return you'll be better off sticking with Infiniti. If you got a problem with this arrangement I can go to your job and tell them how you're lying about your gender and soliciting women for sex at local adult stores."

"Okay Navy, you pulled a fast one on me, I see the lesbianness all up in and through your corneas. This was just a warm-up, next time you'll fold. I'll catch you next time I'm jones'n if you're still employed here that is. Unless you're going to explain all of this to Infiniti, she's going to stick you and me in this same ole room again. So jokes on you baby girl, you have a nice day," Quadette left the room confident and cocky. She was going to get her monies worth one way or another. Now that she had the honors of turning a straight girl inside out, Navy was gonna reap what she just sowed. After five minutes of standing in the toy room, Navy peered around the shelves and corners. She didn't see Quadette in sight nor Infiniti, and she was the only employee on staff. She grabbed the mic of the counter and spoke through the store's intercom system.

"Attention all customers, there's an emergency so Infinity SX will be closing in five minutes please make your final selections and come to the register with your final purchases." Once the last customer checked out, Navy shut down the store, locked up, left the store key in the drop box, took her $1500 dollars, and quit. She hurried up and went to withdraw the $500 from her account before Infiniti could get whiff of her instant resignation. The art of sexual deviancy was not her cup of tea; she was going to leave that up to Infiniti. Infiniti never saw Navy again or Quad. Infiniti's employee turnover was sparse and Navy was the first employee in her chain of stores to ever quit. Still a funny story Infiniti often replayed in her head whenever new employees or new customers entered into her business.

Table of Contents

Chapter 1:Infinite Movements

Kensington Park was one of Infiniti's chill spots, but something felt fishy about chilling today. Infiniti decided to pull up at the park anyway. And just as she had turned the ignition off and was pushing her power window switch down to get some fresh oxygen, she felt the presence of another woman with a piece of steel barricading her window. The woman immediately felt overawed by Infiniti's light gray eyes, long cherry black hair, smooth pecan skin complexion, her cosmopolitan face, and her 5'feet and 6'inches of curves and swerves. Yet and still she had to remain on task.

"I truly admire you Miss Infiniti Brooks, my name is Tame," a stray duckling claimed.

"In my world admire is another word for hate so drop the act baby doll," Infiniti stared straight at the girl and her gun with very daunting eyes.

"Forgive me for invading your privacy, but I got a special gift for you."

"Sorry, but I don't except unspecified gifts from women. And why do you need a gun to give someone a gift unless my gift is death?"

"If your gift was death I would've shot you already."

Instantly Infiniti started snapping her fingers.

"Wait a minute you that lingerie reject who came up in my Woodhaven store with your tub on wheels. I told you I wasn't interested in your lingerie brand. Is this the cold reality of rejection?"

"I'm glad you wasn't interested in my brand because my brand is no longer interested in you. I'm actually here for some other business."

"I parlay alone so give me your gift and scram, and I'll think about opening it."

Tame gave Infiniti a little white box with a Mickey Mouse bow tie neatly tied around it. Momentarily, Tame was out of sight, but she wasn't out of mind. Nobody had ever hounded Infiniti so gravely a day in her life until now. A complement, a gift, a gun, and a stranger didn't mix together, but Infiniti had to know what she was dealing with. She pulled the bow tie loose and popped off the top to a box of nasty maggots. Even though, Infiniti was beyond insulted she laughed hysterically and launched the box of maggots across the grass like she was pitching a fastball.

"I ain't the weak sauce you need to worry about honey because I'm a movement by myself."

The only married man Infiniti was surfing on was this Judge Tatum. Immediately, Infiniti face timed him, but Tatum didn't answer so she shot him a text.

"Tatum you better control your wife before I ruin your marriage and your career.
I don't do drama so you better fly right before I do."

Damn Tatum was busted and he didn't know who to choose. Choice one was Tame and choice two was Infiniti. Those two choices were the two hardest choices in his love life. Somehow Tame got hipped to Tatum's affair with Infiniti. After, Tatum received Infiniti's text he became sweaty like a worker at a sweatshop overseas because he wasn't a juggler. He never had to juggle anything before other then economics and politics. Now his back was against the wall and he couldn't find Tame anywhere. Evidently, she must've left in an utter rush to confront Infiniti, but since she was only a phone call away, he decided to let their phone call be the judge, the jury, and the victim.

-

Digging in her purse, Infiniti pulled out her IPhone. It was one of Infiniti's many men whose name was Harlan.

"What do you want Harlan because I'm not in the talking mood so if you called to whimper about your thot bracket troll you can save it."

Harlan had a girlfriend of three years whom he was very unhappy with. She stopped giving up her juice box and he suspected cheating, but he just couldn't prove it. Instead of just calling a quits he found a woman like Infiniti. Infiniti was actively and passively deviant; the queen of deviancy. Long as the man was pursuing her it was fair game. It wasn't like Infiniti was being unfaithful. She was a woman who didn't want to be committed, didn't have any offspring, or family. There was the family that she knew, the family she didn't know, and the family she didn't want to know, but the few family members she cared about had been killed. She was a 21-year-old woman who was too heartless to catch feelings and could fight or talk her way out of anything, and would fight anyone.

"I just want to take you out Infiniti."

"Don't you have some accounts you should be working on? Why you never wanna take Halo out? I know we got our thing, but you never have date night with your G."

"That somber Susie is never here long enough to say hello to or me to catch her silhouette's shadow on the wall."

"Come get me in an hour then. I was on my way to the Infinity SX store in Farmington Hills."

"You should pick out some sexy lingerie you think I might like for tonight."

"Negro please, you goin love whatever I put on whether it's a uniform or lingerie. Just be on your way."

Infiniti was chauffeured everywhere she went and never came out of her pocket a cent whenever she went out. If a dude was brave enough to mess with her knowing she wasn't nothing, but trouble he had to pay to stay, lay, and play. Wasn't nothing in life for free especially not good, wet, secular vagina. Dudes always throwing they dicks around in a female face when they ask for the little things. It could be a ride to the corner store, DTE, DPL, DPD, or KFC. Soon as the girl shuts the door, dude got his pants unbuttoned, the A/C blowing, and penis in grip pushing down on the girl's neck to give him some head. It's about time a female flipped the tables. She didn't let every Tom, Dick, and Harry in her palace or meet anybody she affiliated herself with. All these jawns needed to know was her phone number and her address.

Infiniti's humble dwelling was in West Bloomfield, Michigan in a 990,000 square foot home that she used her woman skills, get money methods, sugar daddies, and ex-boyfriends to accomplish and accomplice. Her exact address was 7452 Pinewood Trail. It was like the country to her the way her home was surrounded by a bunch of bloom pines and the way that it sat far back beyond the lawn. Her house was only seven years old and probably only had one family resided there prior to her. It had 6 bedrooms, almost 6 bathrooms, a theater room, a curved stairway, Brazilian cherry floors, ten feet ceilings, and many other amazing features that made her home exquisite and deluxe.

Harlan was blowing up her phone, but Infiniti just let it ring.

He answers to me, not me to him.

Infiniti had to make sure the Farmington Hills store was straight and do her routine walk through. Business first, pleasure second. Her key holder there name was Satin, and Satin kept the store and the staff compliant and prepared for a visit. Infiniti was always dressed to stun and infatuate so once she got that "I'm outside" notification she exited the store pleased, but not before she gave Satin a heads up.

"Aye Satin, I'm going out with a friend. I will be leaving my car here so don't think I'm missing."

"Well have a good time and twerk something for me boss lady."

"Y'all twerk and sell these toys."

"We got you boss lady."

When Infiniti propped herself up in Harlan's Yukon hybrid he violated her most important rule like always. He tried to kiss Infiniti on the lips.

"What the hell you doing you know I don't kiss on the lips?" Infiniti pushed Harlan's dimpled, fox red face away from hers.

"Well we've been messing around for four months now. I never had to wait this long for a kiss from my sweet lady."

"Keep dreaming you ain't Tyrese."

Infiniti didn't kiss on the lips because she wasn't anybody's woman. It wasn't that she didn't like to be affectionate, but she wasn't about to be kissing no jawn going home to his mate every night. Lip-kissing was a privilege; a privilege Harlan or any of her other options hadn't earned yet and probably never would.

"So where we headed?"

"We're headed to Chene Park on the Detroit Riverfront. I got us some tickets to a concert I know you're going to love."

-

While Harlan was out and about trying to eat Infiniti like groceries, his girlfriend Halo was out with her side piece Maxwell. Maxwell was a lucky gambler who never lost. For somebody who hated math, he was superb with numbers. He played dice, the lottery, and every game the casino owned. You would think they would've banned him from these places by now, but they haven't. The only major malfunction he had was getting the amount of sex he wanted because he maintained a high sex drive from popping pills, and he opted to get sexed at the most inconvenient times. He popped Mollys, ecstasy, and any pill supplement for a hard-based street drug. Nobody knew he was a pill popper though not even his wife Sunset or his side piece Halo. Only because Maxwell stayed gone all the time and whenever Halo saw him they were in the dark humping somewhere. They couldn't have been paying attention to him because when you're sleeping next to somebody in bed, and looking in their face, you notice things, signs, and red flags. They should've noticed a raised body temperature, sleeplessness, sweating, dilated pupils, loss of appetite etc. They probably thought otherwise, but if only they knew. On the physical tip Maxwell looked like a younger version of the actor Michael Ealy like his identical twin actually which was sad that a person so fine would abuse his body like that.

For the three years Halo has been with Harlan half of those years she spent making herself a slam-piece because even the dude she was cheating with had somebody. Maxwell who she called Max for short was married to an 18-year-old girl named Sunset. They had just gotten married four months ago at the City County Building around the time Infiniti and Harlan met. Maxwell was 29, but he was on that age ain't nothing but a phase tip.

The story with Sunset was simple; young girl who had the world all misconstrued. The only person her body ever knew was Max because he had been messing with Sunset every since she was 15. Maxwell was the pervert that took her virginity, and since she wasn't going anywhere in life anyway she decided to marry the only man who she knew would take care of her. A little game called supply and demand. Coochie is always in demand but sometimes females don't supply it for whatever dumb reason it might be at the time, but Sunset's reason was pregnancy. Morning sickness was kicking her ass everyday preventing her from giving up some of that bomb pregnancy vagina future daddies love too stroke.

Maxwell hit the big game with the deuce of hearts which was his sidepiece who he had been screwing anyway. He just had more reason to screw her now. Halo had always been there for periods, bullshit, arguments, and rollovers. Halo didn't have any reason to be cheating on

17

Harlan besides she was a whore. Bummer, Sunset wasn't wise enough to catch on to her disloyal husband.

Halo drove her Pontiac G5 to spend the night with Max who had got a hotel suite for them. Halo was under the impression Max was going to leave his girlfriend Sunset who had been upgraded to his wife, but that was just the lie to keep her around because Halo had no idea Max had even gotten married. Halo planned to drop Harlan as soon as Max dropped his shorty which was crazy. Every woman says they want a good man, but as you can see that's not true. For some reason Harlan just wasn't good enough for her standards or her walls or her love anymore. She had love for Harlan, but she wasn't in love with him anymore. Maybe if all he would've done is slap her around a little bit even though that wasn't his forte, Max probably wouldn't even be in the picture. Guess she never thought the only thing Max ever wanted her for was sex even though all they ever did was have sex, he gave her money, they had sex, she spent the money, and they had more sex. Wasn't she a good swindler? Going home to Harlan every night and laying up with him like she hasn't been laid up with another man all damn day.

Max and Halo always got an executive suite at the MGM Grand Detroit Hotel especially since he could just go right downstairs and gamble. Downtown Detroit was far enough from his other life or so he imagined, but not too far for him to arrive home promptly. He always stayed there after his casino runs causing him to be their best valued customer. They always gave him a discount, not that he needed it, and excellent service. They always got the same room just for old times' sake Room 347. Halo knocked on the door in a trench coat with nothing under it, but her bare cappuccino skin, and some Marciano Lara heels. Opening the door, Max pulled Halo in and snatched off her trench coat. He didn't have any idea Halo was going to wear a trench coat. And he really didn't have any idea there wasn't going to be anything up under it. Spur of the moment.

-

There was colossal traffic every freeway Harlan got on heading towards Downtown Detroit. The traffic was worst then 5 o'clock traffic on a typical business day. All the cars were bumper to bumper, and as they kept scooting up in traffic still far as hell from their destination, an ambulance and two state troopers bypassed them. Then they started seeing lit flares on the side of the road. Must've been a very bad accident ahead for traffic to be backed up the way it was. Infiniti didn't do traffic so she got on Harlan's head real quick.

"Why the hell are you still sitting here trying to go to that place? Can't you see it's going to be days before we get there?"

"It's not going to be days. Why do you have to be so foul-mouthed every time I try to be genuine to you?"

"Don't get sentimental on me. You know I don't do traffic. It's been a long day why don't we just get a room."

"Well I don't live out here. How was I supposed to know it was going to be an accident?"

"You were supposed to think about it. That's what they got MapQuest for, Google maps, and side streets."

"Sorry I don't think like you."

"Yeah I bet you are." Harlan got off on the nearest exit and made his way to MGM Grand Casino. Since he was gracing the presence of a diva he had to make sure everything he did was ritzy for her. He figured Infiniti would love the casino scene, they had bars, nightclubs, food, and a hotel, and Infiniti could show off that pretty little dress of hers. After a couple of drinks, and a little gambling, Harlan and Infiniti were going to call it a night and book a room at MGM Grand Hotel.

Chapter 2: I Like it Raw

Entering MGM Grand Hotel, Harlan and Infiniti spun to their right where the front desk was. The only problem was there weren't any hotel clerks in sight. Scanning the premises, Infiniti noticed a girl dressed up in business attire with a nametag on chilling on a couch, flipping through a magazine. Then the girl sat the magazine down on a nearby table with a pile of other magazines and started walking like she was about to come check them in. Instead she walked towards the sliding doors, stepped out, gazed around for a moment, walked back in, and then sat back down. The whole time the hotel clerk was staring dead at them, but acted as if they were invisible.

Infiniti nudged Harlan, "please don't tell me this hoe is serious," Infiniti said without whispering. The girl whose nametag read Ally just ignored Infiniti even though she heard exactly what she said.

"Excuse me ma'am," Harlan said courteously looking in the clerk's direction waving his hand.

"Don't say excuse me or wave to that hoe. She ain't blind. Are you on break or something because we need service?"

The girl "Ally" just glanced around like she didn't know who Infiniti was talking too.

"Bitch I'm talking too you!"Infiniti yelled causing Ally to meet eyes with Infiniti.

"For your information this is not my shift and the person you are looking for is late so both you can take a seat and wait until they get here or you can find another hotel to smash at."

"I know customer service is a part of your training and since this is an upscale hotel I advise you to get off your ass and book us a room in 5 seconds or I will personally haul your ass off that couch and behind that counter."

"Excuse me sir you need to teach your girl some manners," Ally crossed her legs.

"Come on Infiniti we can go hit the casino while we wait." Infiniti ignored Harlan and dashed over to Ally and gripped a fist full of her hair and started dragging her on the hotel's marble floors Ally gave in.

"Okay, okay I'll check you in free of charge. Would you like a regular room or a suite?"

"A suite," Infiniti demanded.

Harlan just positioned himself directly behind Infiniti resting his head on her left shoulder. His muscular arms swathed her panty line as her apple bottom riled up his manhood.

"Your room is 348." Infiniti snatched the keys from Ally and headed for the elevators. Once the two got off the elevators and found their room, they couldn't open the door without hearing the guests in the room next door to them.

"Damn they loud as hell. I should make Ally give us another room," Infiniti pondered swiping the key.

"No baby you straight I'm pretty sure you pissed off Ally enough for tonight."

"I was just kidding anyway. That's what hotel rooms are made for right?"

"Right, but maybe they should make sound proof walls because that room right there is ridiculous."

After getting settled in, Infiniti pumped up the AC because things were about to get hot and heavy, then stripped down. Harlan knew what it was so he stripped down to and hit the lights. Harlan and Infiniti was about to get it popping, but their neighbors were making that shit very hard. All Infiniti had to take off now was her heels.

"No keep those on," Harlan pleaded as he saw Infiniti about to unbuckle her lady friends. Trying not to mess up the mood, Infiniti granted Harlan with his one wish for the night.

"Oh my God! Max go deeper," was all you heard. Max had Halo flat on her stomach, legs flat across the bed, clit smoking, reaching for the pillows, squeezing the sheets, lighting her chinchilla up with his ten piece, and her anal up with some booty beads from Infiniti's toy line called "Squirm."

Harlan who could be just as ignorant as Infiniti knocked on the wall.

"Can y'all keep it down in there other people want to hump in peace too," but Max and Halo was too caught up in each other to hear anything.

"Ignore them Harlan, I got a new toy and I want us to try it out."

"What's the name of this toy bay?"

"Pinnacle, we can get the temperatures rising with this nifty little creation." She waved the unopened toy in her hand.

-

Halo was starting to run from Max's thrusts and stiffen up. She was headed for the headboard, but all Max did was follow her.

"I need a break," Halo demanded breathing heavily. You would think she would be use to him by now as many times as she gave up her goodies especially since Max came around frequently.

"You said go deeper so I'm going deeper and deeper." Max smacked Halo on her booty cheeks hard enough to make them clap and sting.

Max's pound game was at an ultimate high since he just popped some pills before Halo came there. Usually he took it easy on her, but since he had extra stamina he couldn't help himself. Max was Halo's second sex partner and you know how dudes get with some tight, ripe cooch.

"Relax!"

"I can't!" Halo rolled over.

"I thought you wanted this. You know exactly what goes down in hotels and hotel rooms. And you came here naked. If you want me too, I can get up and go home to Sunset."

"No don't leave," Halo whined.

"So let me hit those skins how I want too. Let me take your mind off Harlan." That was Halo's soft spot right there Harlan. Halo told Max a bunch of lies about Harlan so that Max would feel sympathy for her. Little did she know Max had his own secret plan. Halo didn't want to get booted out the picture especially since she ruined her relationship for Max. She mine as well give him what he wants.

"Okay have it your way." Max knew he had Halo wrapped around his married finger so he wanted to show her what pain really was. He made Halo get up, bend over with her booty in the air, and touch her toes.

"And you better stay still this time or else." Max sent his chopper so hard and far up Halo's kitty kat she lost her balance and started whimpering.

"Get up Halo you really starting to turn me off!" Max reached down, power slapped Halo, and yanked her to her feet.

Even though Infiniti had Harlan was zoning, the ruckus next door was still aggravating them plus Harlan heard the name "Halo" which wasn't a very popular name.

"I'm sorry bay, but I can't take this BS no more. Harlan didn't put any clothes on. He just walked out the front door and banged on Room 349." It wasn't like it was anything wrong with his body. The most somebody could do was look right maybe even touch if they got close enough, but Infiniti wasn't going to let that happen.

Usually knocks didn't come on Max's and Halo's hotel door. It wasn't like they had room service or maintenance. It wasn't like something got messed up at the front desk and they had to change rooms, or the smoke detectors censors went off. Max wanted whoever was at the door to go away quick and fast so he decided to go ahead and let Halo open it.

"Get up and get the door," Max threw Halo while he sat down on the bed.

"No sit back down I'll get it. I'm just playing hurry up and make it quick."

"But I don't have any clothes on."

"So what! Are you ashamed of your body because I'm not? Ain't like you going anywhere or you dumb enough to stop messing with me for another chump. It's obvious you don't want the chump you got."

Halo was thinking twice about that now, but if she was thinking that hard and was oh so hurt she should've left instead of letting a dude have mind control over you through his hands. Max had never been so aggressive or so vicious to her before, but the abusiveness has always been there whether Halo wanted to admit it or not. She was one of those women who believed when a man hits a woman, they were just expressing their love. She obviously had her definition of abuse all twisted up. Whether a dude put a mark on you or not, abuse is abuse.

Recognizing Halo, Harlan couldn't believe it.

"I knew you were a cunning trick!"

"Trick who you calling a trick? You just as naked as I am!" Still Halo practically fainted. She never thought in her wildest dreams that Harlan would do her dirty even though she deserved it. And to think she told Harlan she wasn't ready when it came to sex like she was a reborn virgin. Halo never thought she would be a heartbeat away from getting caught. She thought all her tracks were untraceable, and she had everything under control, but guilt was about to make her faint. The thought that she could lose Harlan within the next 60 seconds was about to make her faint.

"You told me you weren't ready after that experience you went through, but I knew you were screwing somebody. I guess you've been giving it all to this clown right!" Harlan assumed even though he couldn't see Max. He didn't need to see anybody to know what's been going on.

"You wanted to save yourself for this old cheap creep right who got to take you take a hotel just to smash you!" Max heard a male voice, but that's just to show how much he cares because he didn't get off his buttocks and say nothing in Halo's defense.

"Who the hell are you talking to Halo? You're best friend? Wrap that shit up and come on so we can finish what we started."

"You heard the man go!" Harlan pushed Halo back into her room. He could tell Max wasn't shit just by how he talked to Halo and those fingerprints on her face. Infiniti's impatience self was getting restless so she got up to check up on her bae.

"Please don't go!" Halo begged.

"Don't go? Don't go? What you want me to do join in?"

Infiniti strutted up to Harlan one leg in front of another.

"We're done Halo, go move in with this scrub because you're no longer welcome in my house."

"What a coincidence?" Infiniti heard Harlan say Halo. Halo had sex appeal, but it wasn't enough to compete with Infiniti. You see how quick he told his cappuccino, short, size 3 woman adios. Infiniti had been waiting for this showoff for the longest and wasn't just goin let Harlan go out with a fuck you and have a nice day. Nor was she going to let Halo go out not seeing exactly who her man was sleeping with now.

"Do it to me in front of me." Never had Harlan done anything so spontaneous before. He didn't care about the video cameras nor did Infiniti, nor did he care about how he was about to make Halo feel. It was obvious she didn't give a damn about how he felt so he grabbed Infiniti, threw her into the hallway wall, and began stroking her brains out. Infiniti moaned Harlan's name just to infuriate Halo because on a normal day she was never the one doing the name yelling. Halo just stood there in the door with her mouth open until Mr. Slap a Hoe crept out of the bed. Max saw the bigger picture getting up.

"That's what I'm talking about. I'm trying to get where y'all at," Max rooted tem on pulling Halo out the doorway and slamming the door.

"So you want to watch something?"

"I don't want to watch anything just leave me alone," Halo shut the door, bumping Max like the words excuse e didn't exist and he wouldn't knock the hell out of her ass on the way to the second bed.

"Leave you alone? When are you going to get with the program baby? That was Harlan wasn't it. What's the matter you knew he was cheating right? I mean that's what you told me. And your cheating to so who the hell are you to cry? You obviously single now mine as well get use to the single life because you need me more than ever. I promise to take care of you, house you, and not to slap around if you rock and roll when and how I want too," Max propositioned her, but Halo just sat there completely defeated.

"I know you hear e!"

Once Harlan and Infiniti erupted he carried her back inside the room to the shower there they sexed some more.

Infiniti was leading yet again. Harlan loved the way Infiniti was working him. With Halo out of his life now or so he thought he wanted Infiniti to step up to the plate. If he thought Halo was a heartbreaker, Infiniti sure as hell was going to be the devil himself because Infiniti was not trying to sign up for no relationship not now and maybe not ever. Harlan knew they were just friends with benefits from the get-go, but that must've slipped his mind assuming Infiniti would be down to take it to the next level just because she was down to put on a show for his ex-girl.

Chapter 3: Uptown Knowledge

Whether Halo wanted to accept her new relationship status or not, Harlan was through with her. Through like Boys II Men end of the road through. Of course she had to bone Max until he was snoring with the dream gods, which she brought on herself. She was so motionless after her creep game became disabled. Not even a small abbreviated squeal escaped from her mouth until Max slapped her around again. Then it was moaning, but not the high volume of moaning she was doing at first. The fact that Harlan was with another woman, a pretty woman, in a hotel room that was adjacent to hers was tormenting her the whole time she was banging Max. Apart of her conscience kept telling her, "you know you f'd up right" over and over again. It was nothing wrong with her primary penis, but Halo wanted to seek otherwise so she got what she deserved. Maybe next time she won't take the game for granted because when it comes to love it ain't no second chances. Now Halo's body had a price on it. Maybe next time she'll think about the idiom of "why the chicken did not cross the road."

Harlan and Infiniti were in a snuggly slumber until somebody wouldn't stop beating on the door. Infiniti already knew who it was so she slid on a hotel robe while Harlan stayed in a comatose sleep. Infiniti opened the door and slid into the hallway without giving Halo a chance to speak.

"I could've sworn Harlan got rid of you last night. I guess your sex partner ain't through beating you and your broke back woo-ha up huh?"

"I didn't come here to speak to you."

30

"Actually you didn't come here to speak to anybody. You came here to screw, and now that you got what you wanted you can leave."

"How long have you been in the picture?"

"Long enough to know that you should've been as ancient as an Egyptian pyramid. Maybe you weren't ready, but I stay ready."

"I'm not going to give up on him that easily."

"He's already given up on you so what else do you want because if you want somebody to wipe your tears they made Kleenex for that."

"Oh you're real fancy huh?"

"Have you seen your reflection lately? You got handprints on your face, you just got dumped, kicked out of your house, and it's no telling what kind of other contusions you hiding why you letting a dopey feign play dodgeball with your face. I'll be damned if I let my man solicit another woman in front of me even if I was in the wrong. That just shows that you're a Becky brained floozy."

"I'll be that, but you will see me again and so will Harlan. This ain't over and when we reencounter we'll see who the real refugee is." After saying that Halo dashed off, but no matter how daring her words were only time would be able to tell what she would or wouldn't do.

-

Max snuck out his bedroom before Halo could redirect him. He should've left before the sunrise, but he went to sleep around that time. There was no goodbye kiss or nothing. He just got up, showered, clothed himself, and left his hotel key on the sink for Halo to return when she left. Halo wasn't really sleeping though. She was just lying in the bed with her eyes shut like a mannequin. She wasn't about to stop him from leaving realizing that all this time he was a monster in disguise, eager to slap her around and pimp her body.

Max had to get home to Sunset before her hormones got the best of her and she unleashed a whirlwind of pregnancy rage. As Max turned the key to his 2-story Bloomfield home, he was greeted by Sunset who was wide awake.

"Where the hell you been?" Sunset said out of the blue as Max closed the door.

"I had to make a run baby. What's the matter?" You would think Max was about to knock Sunset on her bottom, but he only treated Halo like crap. He never ever treated wifey bad especially since she grew up in the hood. He knew Sunset wasn't going to back down from nothing.

"You are the matter! You are always the matter! " Sunset pounded her fist into the table.

"You ain't have to make no got damn run all night. What kind of fool do you think I am?'"

"I don't think you're a fool. Why you think you're carrying my son? Why you think I married you? I know I got something good with you and I ain't trying to mess it up. If you don't want to calm down for me, calm down for the baby's sake."

"Calm down nothing. You make that shit sound so good, but I don't buy it. I got two more months to go before I drop this baby and I swear when I do things is going to change around here." Sunset wobbled away frowning as

Max followed her trying to help her up the stairs. He could tell her uterus was hurting and she needed help.

-

Infiniti decided to just let Harlan sleep since nothing seemed to make him snap back to reality and caught an UBER back to her wheels so she could go home. When she arrived at home, she checked her mail, and today was her lucky day because nothing came. She planned to relax until the night rolled around and hit up the Manhattan Club. Infiniti often scouted for girls to work at her various Infiniti SX locations there. She even held a few open interview hiring events there. The last event she held at the Manhattan Club she met this cat named Cardi. He was 26, a DJ at the Manhattan Club, and was sexually depressed. Cardi and Infiniti only had one sexual encounter so far, but anybody could look at Cardi and tell he wasn't depressed no more. Those sex bumps use to be eating his face alive, but now it's as clear as fingernail polish. They will never come back with a woman like Infiniti to fill him up. Cardi had this mystery about him and that was Infiniti's main attraction because Cardi sure as hell wasn't the high roller type Infiniti was use too. It was a bigger adrenaline rush with the unknown then the known. Sometimes it was a good thing to switch it up.

Infiniti gave her clock a fleeting look and the time read 8:00 PM. That was translation for Infiniti get your ass up. The house was quiet since she lived by herself so she started up her laptop, pulled up her playlists, and pressed play. She had speakers everywhere so music filled the house's solitude. Infiniti showered, picked an outfit to slay in, and did a few finished touches and she was ready to bounce.

Not many girls liked to hang out in a female strip joint, but Infiniti was a different breed. Strolling in the club, one of the bouncers who reminded Infiniti of Dwayne "The Rock" Johnson stopped her.

"Where you think you going?" The man put his arm up blocking Infiniti like she couldn't get in the club.

"Excuse me?" Infiniti didn't expect anybody or anything to prolong her process.

"I mean you ain't going nowhere until you hand over those seven digits." Even though the bouncer was cute, her mind was focused on Cardi. Lucky for her the bouncer dropped his arm so Infiniti could walk straight in at her own will.

"Okay but all you had to do was ask, give me your hand." Once the bouncer gave Infiniti his hand she dug in her handbag, and grabbed her eyeliner and wrote *kiss my ass* on the man's palm. The bouncer actually thought he had a number until he read his hand. It was too late for him to have a reaction because Infiniti was already inside the club. She directed her attention to Cardi when she spotted him on the turntables. She started winking at him, but then a dark, auburn skinned bony chick joined him, and started tonguing him down in the mist of their wink sequence. Now if it was a kiss on the lips then maybe miss thang could pass as a friend, but it wasn't an ordinary kiss that had to be his girlfriend. Once miss thang was out of sight she made her move.

"Hi stranger. If I was a kisser I'll probably tongue you down too, but I'm not so what you think about a hug?"

"That's cool," Cardi hugged Infiniti tightly.

"Can you name a day when you ain't looking good or smelling good?"

"Good isn't the word I would use, but I can't."

"So when we goin hook up again?"

"We getting straight to the business I see. I must have a time limit I see."

"You ain't got no damn time limit, what makes you think that?"

"Baby girl wasn't kissing you like that for no reason. She must be wifey or close to it," Infiniti continued talking over music and seeing miss thang surface."

"Maybe she is, maybe she's not."

"Look I already put two and two together so go ahead and fess up. You're not going to blow your chances with me." Infiniti ended about to walk off until she felt Cardi's arm hold her back while his broad was sulking it all in and on her way to confrontation central.

"Excuse me you kind of close to my man and the only chick that's goin be all up in his face is me."

"Calm down Dakota it ain't even like that." Little did Dakota know it was like that. It was straight like that.

"I'm not trying to take your man sweetie and if you bae why you questioning me? I'm just a regular citizen in a strip club talking to a DJ. What could we possibly have to talk about with you breathing down our necks? I don't think your man is dumb enough to flaunt me round in your face do you?"

Dakota glanced at Cardi, "no."

"So what's the problem?"

"There ain't no problem anymore." Dakota walked away.

"Damn baby you good."

"There you go with that word again. You need to learn you some synonyms starting now." Infiniti departed to the bar to find a girl balling in tears.

"Bartender let me get an Electric Long Island Ice Tea."

Infiniti looked the emotional girl up and down that was next to her wondering what the hell she was doing in the club boo-wooing. She looked more like she wanted to have a pity party with some Baskin Robbin's ice cream, but she was really just a con artist high on emotion.

"You look like a black Pocahontas," Infiniti complemented the girl who actually did look like one with her black complexion, long eyelashes, her little face, and her long black hair that touched her crack. It was in her head so it was hers.

"Why aren't you in the bathroom or something? Don't nobody want to see you weeping around here. Don't you know how quick dudes can spot a weak link? You better get yourself together because your tears will lure a bunch of heartless clowns over here who say they want to comfort you, but that's just game right there."

"Everything was fine earlier until me and my boyfriend broke up. I don't understand why we broke up. I didn't even do nothing." The girl slammed her head back down in her hands when she finished explaining her frustration. Her and her so called boyfriend really did break up, but she was just using the whole crying scheme to her advantage to see who it could be a magnet for. She knew when a dude was spitting game to her and when he wasn't. She was just trying to meet somebody new. She was just trying to meet somebody new being new to the city and all. She didn't expect the first person she met to be somebody who seemed a lot like her.

"If y'all broke up why are you crying? I'll rather be single then tied down any day."

"We were so happy though, than another female answered his phone and told me she was his girl. All that time he was just using me." The girl kept the conversation going playing roles with Infiniti. She was a female hustler herself. She just hadn't gotten a chance to recruit anybody else to her team yet, and the one person she did have, she found herself catching too many feelings for. Lucky for her, his girl pulled a fast one so she could snap out of it. The girl felt she'll keep the reindeer games going since Infiniti appeared to be a sociable person that would probably show her around.

"You need to wake up and smell the black coffee. You need to start using that body of yours to your advantage and let the amenities of life make elate you because it's obvious you can't handle love."

"My name is Tierney, but people just call me Tier. What's your name?" The girl asked straightening up her face and lifting her head up playing Infiniti like a board game.

"Infiniti and I would be flattered to teach you a couple things," Infiniti said sliding her shot glass to the bartender for another shot.

"Can you stand up for a minute?" Infiniti twirled the girl around in a circle. You would've sworn she was bi, but she was nowhere near it. She was just trying to see Tier's body metrics and by the looks of it money signs were written all over Infiniti's face.

"You would do that? I mean you seem like you know what you're talking about. I was going to say that earlier," Tier claimed sitting back down.

"As long as you want to learn, I'll teach."

"Okay you talking real good."

"I ain't just talking though, but I'm a let you know right now I'm a teach you how to manipulate dudes with your body so when the next chump come around, ain't no way in hell you should let him get the cookie for free. And if anything he'll be crying because soon as you get what you want from him, you'll be onto the next one."

"I feel you, but won't I be considered a gold-digger then or something like it?" Tier acted innocent like those words offended her. Like she didn't have a list of how many hearts she broke, girlfriends she's replaced, marriages she's dismantled, and friendships she's shattered. Tier had screwed over more than half the population in her city which brought her up here to get a fresh start, and start her list over. As Infiniti talked more and more she knew it was going to be a piece of cake for her to take over this city since she was going to be dealing with a prototype of her if not worse.

"No you will be considered a realist. If your more worried about how somebody is going to classify you, you ain't ready to know what I know," Infiniti began to leave her stool.

"Please don't go, I just moved up here from Sugar Land, Texas and I really don't know anybody. I could really use a friend and some uptown knowledge," Tier pleaded.

In Infiniti's mind she was pimping this girl and that's exactly what she was going to do. But who was she fooling; Infiniti didn't have enough time to pimp nobody. *I guess I can make time to school her.* Writing down her number on the back of an old receipt she had in her purse, Infiniti knew she hit the jackpot tonight so she thought.

"Call me when you ready for your lessons." Tier took Infiniti's number with the biggest smirk anybody could wear on their face. Too bad Infiniti didn't notice. Tier knew these lessons were going to be effortless because little did she know, Tier was just like her.

In the dressing room all the strippers could tell Dakota wasn't herself.

"What's the matter?" Tamale asked.

"I don't think I satisfy Cardi and I think he's going to cheat on me if he already hasn't."

"Satisfy what you mean you don't satisfy him? Either you giving it up or you ain't so which one is it," another stripper commented.

"Shut up Spicy! Don't answer that question. You should know better telling everybody your bedroom business. You never know who might use it against you. And you know Cardi don't want nobody, but you. He certainly won't give none of us no play."

"What?"

"Just joking, don't you know a joke when you hear one?" Tamale wasn't joking though. Almost every female that worked or walked up in the club tried to flirt with Cardi, but he always shot them down. He wasn't about to fool around with none of the strippers there because he didn't do strippers. Not to mention he knew Dakota would find out about him messing around faster then she would if he messed around with a girl on the street.

"I guess I'm tripping huh."

"Yeah unless you know something we don't."

"It was nothing I just saw him talking to some girl earlier and that was all I could think about."

"What girl?"

"I don't know her name."

"And what did you do?"

"I confronted him, but she made some good points so I backed off."

"Better go check on him."

"I will in a minute."

Going back up to the DJ booth Infiniti toyed with Cardi some more.

"Did you think of a new word yet?"

"Try a sentence, I love your swag."

"Well if you love my swag then I know you're going to love what I'm thinking. Never mind, I forgot your girl patrolling you like five-o, you ain't goin be down," Infiniti teased Cardi reeling him into her trap.

Chapter 4: Shoeboxes and Locks

Blowing time at her ranch home in Whitmore Lake, Tame found three size 10 and half Nike shoeboxes in Tatum's closet planted behind his suits and ties. They were loaded with toxic evidence that confirmed Tame's infidel beliefs. Now the hours Tatum claimed were office hours made sense because he was gone real tough, unusually tough, cheater tough for months.

Maybe Tatum didn't think Tame was the inspector type. Maybe Tatum was prepared to get caught. Whatever the case was, Tame had to do some explorations of her own. One box had nothing, but receipts from every mall and restaurant you could think of. Another shoebox had last year's checkbook with a bunch of checks written out to a woman named Infiniti Brooks. It also had Western Union and MoneyGram stubs to the Infiniti chick too. The third shoebox had a bunch of brand new female and male sex toys from Infiniti's toy line. Tatum brought the toys to support her business because they never used them just like they never had sex. He was still a creep rookie. He wasn't really comfortable with cheating sexually, but a cheater is a cheater. He just loved Infiniti and valued their time since Infiniti made him smile and Tame gave him migraines. Infiniti's smiling wasn't going to last for long because she was a sex addict. As nice as money was with no play, she wasn't having it. Sex always came first, and money always came second. Tatum was just one of those married men who wanted a younger woman he could blow his executive money on.

Tame didn't cry though nor did she panic. She was 25 and she figured only a young lent ball could make a married man do something so senseless. She figured she'll have some fun on her own because her wedding vows were eternal. Once Tame made a mockery out of Infiniti and

Tatum realized exactly what Tame was capable of, if he ever cheated he would be bowing down to Tame and never cheat again.

The little episode at the park was just the beginning, Tame lucked up that day. Infiniti had just left Tatum's house before she came to the park, and when Tatum left the house, Tame peeked out the window, grabbed her keys, and sat in her car waiting for Infiniti to pull off so she could tailgate her. Lucky for her, Infiniti didn't pull off until Tatum was completely in the house so it wasn't hard for Tame to keep up. Even though Tame had no idea where she would end up when Infiniti's car stopped, she wasn't about to turn around. When Infiniti pulled into the park, Tame knew it was time for her introduction. The maggots' idea she had gotten from a throwback show on TV. It's the 20th century, don't nobody play by the books no more. You have to be witty and creative. Tame knew Infiniti living the life she lived would be going crazy getting a gift box from a strange woman. Infiniti going to the park just made it easy for Tame to start playing her dose of mind games.

-

Just about to slip Cardi off to the back of the club, Infiniti was thrown off by the owner Carmella who came screaming all up in his grill like his momma. That was such a turnoff.

"I just saw the cameras are you retarded?"

"What's the issue now Carmella?"

"You don't need to be associating with anybody I do business with. Infiniti is off limits so keep your paws off of her. You already got me and Dakota what more do you need?" Carmella claimed rubbing her leg against Cardi's and grabbing his sack.

"Me and you are done so you can cut that out right now! I don't care what you and Infiniti got going on and don't act like you care about Dakota because you don't. If you did you wouldn't be screwing me now would you!" As much as Carmella fronted about Cardi fucking around on Dakota, she was really more concerned about Cardi messing around on her. She was just as bad as anyone else and worst because they were banging on the side and she was a jealous woman. She had made many passes at Cardi before when Cardi and Dakota use to live under her roof and finally she succeeded right before they got their own place. Cardi was waxing her walls on a regular basis especially since their secret came with benefits. Carmella was the one who got Cardi the DJ gig at the club because it was her club and she handled the firing and hiring. Not to mention she was always throwing Cardi some money. Guess his pipe had some money signs on it. It's a shame, but Cardi and Carmella had been sleeping around on the side five months before he met Infiniti. Since Cardi couldn't bear sticking his future aunt by marriage any longer, and couldn't bare letting Dakota find out, him and Dakota moved out. Only now Carmella was whipped and Infiniti was the broad Cardi wanted to knock off.

"Stop lying to yourself. Ain't nothing over especially not between me and you. I ain't goin wait forever. You better start effing me again because if you don't you mine as well move to another country because if my people find you it ain't goin be pretty." Carmella was divorced so she didn't have a full-time man in her life. All her nephews were gang-related and she would sick them on Cardi if she couldn't get her way. In the meantime Cardi searched the atmosphere for Infiniti, but Infiniti was long gone about to find her another victim of her sex crimes.

At the nearest stoplight Infiniti looked over to her left and saw a '15 Maserati GranSport and a fine Jamaican brother driving it. Her eyes weren't playing tricks on her and she definitely knew a race when she saw one. He was part Cherokee Indian and part Jamaican. It was no way she was going to let Mr. Showtime pass her by. Little did she know Mr. Showtime had already got a whiff of her pixie dust. Mr. Showtime rolled down his window letting out all the ganja smoke he was inhaling and exhaling while Infiniti was checking out his stats. He had a nice low cut. He looked to be around 32, he had chilly skin, skin that could give you the chills just looking at it. He looked very, very Infinitiable. Right after he turned down his Jamaican music he spoke up.

"Do you got ante plans for da nite?" Mr. Showtime asked sending chills up Infiniti's spine with his patois accent.

"Not at the moment, but I would love to partake the night with you."

"Cum den." Following behind Mr. Showtime Infiniti switched lanes every time he did until they ended up at a gated area that led to a private estate that sat further back. Afterwards, Mr. Showtime led Infiniti in his palace.

"I know you can't possibly live here alone." Infiniti glanced around in amazement because his property was ten times better then hers. She felt like she was on an island because the walls were painted Caribbean colors, and there were big, monumental paintings, and tall tropical plants everywhere.

"I don't."

"So why would you bring me to your house so your girl can come home to us in the nude?"

"Who say we getting naked?"

45

"I did," Infiniti teased coming out of her clothes as Mr. Showtime was leading her up a double stairwell.

"You're so blunt and outspoken. I like dat."

"And you're tall, muscular, and handsome. I like that too."

"Are you always dis friendly following strange men like me home?"

"No usually they follow me."

"I see you got a sense of humor too," Mr. Showtime commented as him and Infiniti finally made it to a canapé bed and a guest room."

"So what's your name?"

"My name is Gunz." Infiniti wondered what that name met since it sounded like a street given name. She hoped it didn't have anything to do with guns, but she wasn't trying to get to know him like that at least not yet. She was thinking more about freaking this incredible man she had in front of her right now. And when she saw that his pipe was standing up in his pants she knew she was about to give him the business. She had never had any Jamaican penis before, but she loved to try new things. Shit she saw the movie Belly.

"I guess you haven't gotten your socks knocked off lately."

"Or maybe I know a fine queen when I see one."

"I feel that just give me one word to describe your sex life?"

"Empty."

"My name is Infiniti and I promise you'll never have to say that again." When Gunz and Infiniti stood up neck and neck, he had no idea how Infiniti was about to whip her treasure chest on him. Infiniti threw Gunz against the wall and became more flexible then a Chinese woman. She mounted her leg on Gunz's shoulder and pounded her walls at his joystick. Then she popped her walls up against his dangler as he held her legs in the air. Gunz was just blown away and had came off every position so far.

"Damn you are one hell of a queen."

"Shut up and take it," Infiniti exalted while twirling around Gunz's woodpecker.

"Can your girl do this?"

"She can't do none of dis." Gunz didn't hesitate.

"Why ain't she sexing you right? All you want is this tight, ripeness right?"

"I got you now right?" Infiniti knew she had Gunz right where she wanted him. After both Infiniti and Gunz splashed a couple more times, they talked for a minute and Infiniti left. Looking at her phone she saw that Harlan had called. *Should I call him back seeing as though he probably does need some TLC right now? Nope I had my fun for the night. I think I'll just go home and lay it down.*

-

Too bad Harlan wasn't going to sleep no time soon. When he reached home which was a custom brick walled lakefront house in Novi from his hotel stay he called a locksmith and got the locks changed. Good thing some of their jokers were 24 hour locksmiths. If Halo would've came straight home after she left the hotel and would've stayed at home then maybe she could've avoided this situation. Since she came home and changed her clothes, left, and never came back she had to suffer for her careless thinking. Halo was screaming and cussing, and banging on the doors for hours while Harlan just sat in the living room looking dead at her.

"You cheated on me too you know," Halo kept telling herself.

"Yeah I did because I knew you were doing me dirty!"

"Can you at least give me some clothes?" Harlan went up to their bedroom, opened their bedroom window and started tossing Halo's clothes, shoes, purses, and jewelry at her then he went downstairs and turned on the sprinklers. Halo just opened up her car trunk and started loading all her stuff up in disbelief, but wasn't shit she could do. She was outside looking in instead of inside looking out. Like she told Infiniti this was nowhere near over. When Halo got all her stuff off the wet grass she sat in her car, in her now wet, wrinkly clothes with her wet stringy hair. Good thing she had a perm because otherwise her hair would've been a poofy, nappy disaster. She called her older sister even though she really didn't want too. It didn't seem like Tame was going to answer the phone at first, but finally she did.

"Hello," Tame cleared her sleepy voice.

"Tame I need somewhere to crash for a while, Harlan then put me out."

"That's not my problem Halo you shouldn't have did whatever you did. I'm married now so I ain't got no public housing for you. Ain't no female coming in here because they don't know how to control they man and they hit a bridge in their relationship so they can sleep with my man."

"But Tame I'm family, I'm not just anybody. You don't even know what happened for you to automatically assume it's my fault. And why do you think everybody is out to get Tatum? I don't want him; I just want a place to lay my head."

"I would say it ain't no hard feelings, but then I would be lying. I just don't want to put myself in a predicament I'm going to regret."

"Tame please I'm begging you! You don't know how I feel sitting in front of this man's house like this. I need to know if I got to go left or right."

"You can stay for two weeks, but after that you got to go. If you don't leave I will drag you and your rags to my curbside do you understand?"

"I understand." Halo hung up the phone a little content. Maybe this quality time she was about to spend with her sister was going to refurbish their sisterhood. Since Tatum was sleep, Tame didn't disturb him even though he would have a rude awakening in the morning. Tame was a very private person who kept to herself. She never hung out with any girlfriends, and didn't have other wives calling their house to talk shit about their husbands behind their back. She knew people yeah no doubt, but she lived a boring life and she was proud of it. Tame knew when Tatum saw Halo he would know something was drastically wrong. Nobody Tame knew had barely been in their house before let alone spent the night. Tame was surprised Halo out of all people, sister or not, remembered where she stayed.

Briefly after Tame's and Halo's phone call ended, Tame waited for Halo downstairs because she knew if she would've stayed laying in the bed she would've dozed back off. That would've took her longer to open the door, and that would only make Halo ring the doorbell more which would wake up Tatum and then it was definitely going to be a problem. A problem that Tame wanted to avoid until tomorrow.

When Tame opened up her door and saw Halo's face, her wet clothes, and wet hair she couldn't believe it.

"Have you been scrapping and playing in the sprinklers?"

"I don't want to talk about it thank you."

"Well go to the guest room and get some rest. Take a shower too, and we'll talk about it in the morning." Tame pointed actually concerned about what was really going on with her sister. The nicer Tame that is because the Tame that was just on the phone was just plain old snide.

Chapter 5: 2 fine 2 whine

Attempting to arise first, Tatum shot up so he could go serve some law and justice before Tame could detect his dearth. He was one of the creepers too. Heading for a morning piss he saw a body occupying one of their guest rooms. Since his lovely wife didn't inform him of any visitors, he attempted to creep on in the room to get a closer look at Halo who was asleep without any sheets just a plush bra and a plush thong. Tatum hadn't seen Halo since a couple years back before Tame and her fell out. He could barely recognize her with that matured body she owned because she had sprouted all up. Tame and Halo fell out because Tame didn't invite Halo to her wedding. Halo was fuming at Tame for a long time, but eventually they made a truce still never being as tight as they use to be.

Just as Tatum was about to attack his prey, Tame came along.

"Is Halo awake yet?"

"That's who that is? I can't believe I'm hearing this. I really can't believe she's in our house. When did y'all reunite? Last time I checked y'all relationship had flat lined. Not to mention you never have company. I guess y'all got some kind of secret thing going on. What you be sneaking her in the night and out in the morning? I wasn't supposed to know or something?"

"Shut up! And none of your damn business! What you thought me and my sister was going to be arch enemies forever?"

"You didn't even invite her to our wedding and now she's spending the night?"

"She's not the one I don't trust; that person is more like you. My sister is precious to me and if you ever put your hands on her I will kill you with my bare hands. That's why I didn't invite her because I don't want you to come near her or get close to her. Have her thinking your Mr. Perfect when we both know how rotten you are."

"Damn I didn't know you felt that way. Maybe you should tell Halo to put some real pj's on with a man like me in the house then."

"Don't worry I got my sister covered, but how about your tracks?"

"Look I got some judge business to handle so we can do the whole argument thing later." Tatum showered and got dressed in a True Religion outfit with some basic all white forces, and went off to Infiniti's house for their Thursday lunch which included some conversation, food, and Infiniti's weekly allowance, but Infiniti was still knocked out. Tatum called Infiniti to tell her he was on the way. Finally, she heard the phone ringing and ranging.

"Hello."

"I know you ain't still sleep?"

"Once Infiniti heard the sound of Tatum's crispy voice she sat up realizing today was her payday."

"No I was just trying to make sure you were still coming before I went and got all dolled up."

"Well I'm on my way so I'll see you in a few."

"Alright then I'll be waiting." Infiniti took a 5 minute shower and dived in her closet so she could find something short and quick. She came out with a skirt and short set on like always with the matching stilettos. Infiniti could see her crinkles were turning into waves, but either way it went her hair wasn't rundown so she fidgeted with it a little bit and kept it moving. Knowing Tatum was about to be pulling up any minute Infiniti threw on some Cartier ear rings and frames, a Chanel handbag, and went to the door. By the time Infiniti locked both locks, Tatum was right there in the driveway.

"Hi, Tatum, "Infiniti greeted her light hazel emperor. His hazel golden eyes were just as golden as his sunlit skin looking seven years younger then what he really was.

"It's always a pleasure to see you." After riding in Tatum's black Cadillac SRX Crossover for about 25 minutes, Infiniti and him ended up at Bahama Breeze.

-

Halo woke up in the nuisance of Tame trying to break her laptop keyboard with her fist. Halo threw on a robe Tame had laid out in the guest room closet for visitors and walked into the den as she listened to Tame talk out loud.

"Damn she's a little smart wench!" Tame was online trying to see if Infiniti's number was listed in the white pages, but it wasn't.

"Who's a smart wench?" Halo wondered.

"I haven't really consulted with anybody yet about my problem and I don't know if I should tell you. I think it would be better left unspoken."

"You think I'll rat you out?"

"Desperate causes calls for desperate measures."

"What is it going to take for you to trust me?"

"I'm sorry Halo, but I don't trust anybody not even Tatum."

"And that's what I don't understand. I'm not just anybody I'm your sister, your only sister, your flesh and blood."

"I'll rather protect you then make you a confidant."

"Protect me from what?"

"People like Tatum. Maybe if you weren't so easy you wouldn't attract all the dumb scumbags you rock with."

"I can't deal with this right now," Halo turned her back.

"By the way the only one who's going to be caught around this house naked is me so you better start sleeping like its 10 degrees in this house unless you got somewhere else you rather stay."

-

Lifting a pillow in the air Dakota was about to smother Cardi until he woke up gasping for air because he was having a vulgar dream. Once Dakota noticed Cardi's erect penis she thought about hopping on it and opening her vulva up without any of Cardi's help, but she was too scary. The whole idea of Dakota taking over in the bedroom was just a thought that would never escalate any further then the corners of her mind. All of a suddenly words started falling out of his mouth. One word to be exact which was "Infiniti." Cardi kept saying Infiniti's name for like an hour, and all Dakota did was sit there with folded arms like he could see how angry she was. Getting up Dakota stormed down the carpeted stairs of their authentic townhome, reached in the freezer, grabbed 2 sausage biscuits, and warmed them up in the microwave. Dakota was a good one to be thinking about food when her man was laying in her bed daydreaming about another woman. By the time Dakota ate up her mini breakfast her conscience had gotten the bitchness out of her and replaced it with some balls of steel. Dakota turned the cold water on in the bathtub and let it run aimlessly for 20 minutes before she filled a bucket up to the rim. Standing besides Cardi she poured half of the water out on Cardi who start shivering like he was standing naked in the middle of Antarctica on an icecap.

"What the winter?" Cardi was shocked.

"This bucket is still half full so I advise you not to tick me off anymore."

"I was only sleep, shit what did I do?" Cardi didn't know what to do. He didn't know if Infiniti called or came by there or if Dakota had heard something through the grapevine or if he was finally getting punished for his affair with Dakota's aunt. He didn't want to tell a white lie if it wasn't going to get him out of trouble.

"I don't know no damn Infiniti!"

"Who the hell are you talking too like that," Dakota poured the rest of the water on Cardi.

"Maybe that will help you learn some respect." Out of nowhere Cardi's phone started ringing.

"You better hope it's not that hoe you were dreaming about calling you." Cardi couldn't even move to reach his phone. He was so cold. The covers he had covering his body wasn't doing him any justice either because they were soaked now. Guess maybe he'll think twice about sleeping half naked around Dakota. Quickly, Dakota grabbed Cardi's phone off the nightstand and pressed speaker.

"Who the hell is this?"

"Is this Dakota?"

"And you then told the hoe my name," Dakota was heated talking too Cardi who needed to go lay up in a hot tub somewhere.

"Who you calling a hoe, this is your aunt little girl so you better watch your mouth before I make you rinse it out with some soap." Dakota was so embarrassed.

"I'm sorry aunt. I thought this was somebody else."

"Yeah I bet you did. Is everything with you and Cardi okay?" Carmella asked for her benefit figuring Cardi and her were on bad terms and he would love her and only her one day.

"We're fine it was just a misunderstanding," Dakota lied. Cardi just sat fixed in the bed glad Dakota answered the phone so he didn't have to talk to Carmella who was starting to act stalkerish and obsessive. How was they supposed to keep anything on the down low if Carmella was dropping hints like an impulsive killer? It wasn't like Carmella had any business calling Cardi anyway. Dakota had a cell phone and Carmella was Dakota's aunt only, and Carmella didn't need to talk to Cardi about nothing concerning the club. Weren't no birthdays or holidays coming up. Guess Carmella was getting real gutsy and was about to make-up some shit.

"Something told me to call you guys. I tried to call your phone, but something was wrong with it. I was wondering if Cardi could come move these boxes for me out the basement. I'm going to remodel it and there in the way." Carmella didn't need Cardi to move no damn boxes that was just the lie. Cardi was saying no over and over again in his head. Lucky for him Dakota had his back.

"I'm sorry aunt, but we're busy right now so can you find somebody else?" That was not what Carmella wanted to hear, but she had to deal with it.

"Okay I guess so, but if he gets free then tell him to come on over."

"I sure will," Dakota hung up. Cardi was saying yes over and over in his head now.

"I'll be keeping your phone with me until I want to give it back," Dakota claimed flying out of the room and leaving Cardi alone.

-

For lunch Tatum and Infiniti ordered Jamaican grilled chicken wings and grilled chicken cobb salad.

"So how's the wife been?"

"Tame is still the same evil being she always been, and I don't know if things are going to get worst or better now that her sister Halo is back around." Either Tatum was starting to get to comfy around Infiniti or he had just let Tame and Halo's names slip out of his mouth, but she wasn't expecting Tatum to mention any names. He never revealed any names before. Not that he spoke in code, but he never talked about what went on in his household which was a plus for Infiniti because she didn't want to hear about that shit. That was such a turnoff to sit up and listen to a guy talk about his spouse in front of her face. She only asked to be polite, just to see what the feedback was going to be, but she really didn't want that type of conversation. She wasn't there to listen or counsel. She was there to make them blackout for a minute and block out everything and everyone outside of her which Tatum had yet to conquer that tactic. It was weird for Infiniti not to have tried anything because she didn't have a problem with being the aggressive one, but not today. Tatum was too fine to keep whining about his wife. Infiniti knew he was missing what every man complaining about his wife was missing. If he wanted advice then he should really look into getting a shrink. Where were earplugs when you needed them? When she heard the name "Tame" she thought about the day in the park. And when she heard the name "Halo" she thought of Harlan. Infiniti didn't have a clue what the hell she was getting herself into even though it was a little bit too late to pullout the situation. Her motto was "never get involved in something you can't handle" and as far as she was concerned she could handle anything.

Chapter 6: No Pleasure, No Paradise

Officially 34 weeks gestation, Sunset presumed she was experiencing Braxton Hicks contractions until her contractions started getting real. They started getting more powerful and blasting through her body more recurrently. This was no false alarm so Max called 911 so EMS could get the job done. While Sunset was laying there throbbing, she started thinking about all the people that wasn't going to be in her baby's life. The only people her baby was really going to see was mommy and daddy.

Sunset's old best friend Lana whose nickname was "Lola" was going to be the baby's godmother, but that was past tense. Fortunately, Max claimed Lola was trying to smash him and was jealous of Sunset because of all the lavish things that Max spoiled her with. The jealousy Sunset could understand because only rich people live the way she was living, but the smashing part she couldn't. Of course Sunset took Max's side which made sense because he was the main and only provider in her life. She didn't even bother to ask Lola about her suspicions, she just stop talking too her especially since she was already acting stank towards Sunset. It was definitely reasons behind the madness of why Lana was acting stank. She knew what kind of things Sunset would have to endure dating an older man, and she knew it wasn't worth it. Sunset was already beginning to lose sight of the important things most people accomplish in their early years like getting a full education. A real man would never want to be with a woman without any book smarts. Sunset still hadn't even graduated from high school yet nor was Max even trying to persuade her to finish. The ill feeling that Max ignited between Lana and Sunset was only to cause division in their friendship and keep Sunset all too himself.

"What is taking them so long?"

"Baby it's only been a couple of minutes."

"Well, it feels like it's been forever."

"I'm pretty sure they're on their way."

"Call them and see," Sunset cried breathing deeply. There was obviously no way to win anything with a pregnant woman in labor or any woman so Max just gave up. Lucky for him EMS was reversing up the driveway. Max stood by Sunset's side as they loaded her up in the ambulance, but once he got the hospital information he was gone. He was gone to take care of his favorite two addictions. Heading for his pill stash he hit up the refrigerator for an Ice Mountain bottled water and popped two pills. Even though Max's baby wasn't shy from being born into the world; it was one of those times when he had his mind on other things; more like a person. He couldn't stop contemplating about the main person that has been fulfilling him lately. The fact that his baby was going to be premature didn't even cross his mind or the fact that there could be serious complications in general. The umbilical cord could be wrapped around the baby's neck cutting off circulation, doctors might have to perform an emergency C-section, or the baby could be breached. Despite those pretenses, Max was not worried about it. EMS just closed the doors after securing Sunset inside and took off.

"Do you see my husband behind us?" Sunset kept asking one of the EMT's after they timed her contractions which were four minutes apart, checked her vital signs, and listened to the baby's heartbeat.

"What kind of vehicle does he drive?"

"He drives a '15 royal blue Tange LS."

"No I don't see any sign of him."

"Where the hell could he be while I'm having his baby?"

"Maybe he's already at the hospital."

"And maybe you just want me to ram my foot up your ass." At first the EMT didn't take it offensive because women in labor often say things they don't mean out of pain. Sometimes they meant what they said, sometimes they didn't even remember half of the things they said. Sometimes it was just the pain talking, but the EMT would've been better off if she didn't pay Sunset any mind.

"I was just trying to help."

"Help? How can you possibly help me, but tell me to breathe, relax, it's going to be okay. Here's a newsflash that shit doesn't work not even on TV!"

"Your baby doesn't need any stress now.""

"Do you have a baby?" Sunset boldly asked the EMT which hit home because she was a lesbian.

"You don't know shit about me okay!" In response, the poor EMT started balling her eyes out. The other EMT who hadn't said a word since he spoke to Max patted the girl on the back.

"Hello, I'm the one that's pregnant and you don't see me crying," Sunset complained caressing her belly.

-

Dialing Halo, the only thing that Max could think about now was some puss. When Halo's phone started ringing she wanted it to be Harlan so bad she answered it as fast as she could.

"Hello."

"Where you at I'm about to come get you?" Immediately, Halo caught an attitude.

"And take me where?"

"To my house."

"You never took me to your house before what changed?"

"Look I'm trying to give you this money, but you got to earn it." Max knew that would be the magic words. Money sounded real good right now especially since Harlan or Tame wasn't going to be breaking her off anytime soon. Even though, Halo was still disgusted at the way Max had treated her the night at the hotel, Halo gave into the side of her that wanted to get away from her sister, and feel a man's touch.

"I'm over my sister's house." Max didn't even know Halo had a sister especially since Halo never talked about her, but that shows how much they didn't know about each other.

"Now all of a suddenly you have a sister. All this time we've been sneaking around and in these red-handed predicaments, and it never occurred to you that your sister could come in handy."

"Actually my sister and I don't even get along that's why I never mentioned her. Not that you ever asked me about my personal life besides about Harlan. And Harlan knows that we don't get along so therefore she is off limits."

"Well, where does she stay?"

"She stays in Whitmore Lake. Just hop on 1-696 going west and I'll give you more directions when you get closer."

"Bet I'm on my way." Tame saw Halo getting ready and she had that sister intuition.

"I hope you not about to go hang out with that buster who put them marks on your face."

"For the record these are sex scars. He didn't mean to do it, but I like it rough, and if you think these scars are something you should see the ones I put on his back."

"Shut up Halo I'm not stupid! And I know they certainly didn't come from Harlan because if they did you wouldn't be kicked out of his house right now so who else you boning now?"

"I would appreciate it if you wouldn't mention Harlan's name right now," Halo tussled with her shirt.

"Why I doubt Harlan did anything wrong?" Which was true, but Halo decided to go ham on Tame just for being a know it all.

"I didn't tell you shit about me and Harlan's relationship so you can keep your ignorant ass thoughts to your damn self!"

"I would start doing a lot more ass kissing and stop acting so over-sensitive because you're going to need me more than you ever needed me if you keep living the way you living now."

"Whatever," Halo bumped past Tame noticing she missed a call which was Max so she finished navigating him to her. Ten minutes later she took a look out the front picture window and saw his whip which was her q to go.

Soon as Halo got in the car Max unbuttoned his jeans, whipped his kielbasa out, and pushed Halo's head towards his shaft as he took off to his house. He was going to complete his dome with some nookie. Halo didn't even let-up she just surrendered herself completely.

-

While Halo was swallowing Max's precum, Sunset was swallowing pain alone in her hospital room. Sunset swore when the day came that she would give birth, she would get every drug she could get but, drugs were pointless. She didn't have anybody to squeeze or hold her hand, nobody to fluff her pillows, nobody except the doctors and the nurses. Sunset was dilated seven centimeters already and feared the worst. She prayed Max would show his face. He had turned all of Sunset's friends against her so it wasn't like she could count on any of them. Although, true friends would be the first ones to be there for you no matter how mad at you or how mad at them you were. Even though, babies were the new trend this day and age, Sunset's family just couldn't sit with Max's and Sunset's age difference. That's one of the reasons why Sunset and Max didn't have a big wedding because even if they sent out beautiful wedding invitations, they didn't have any supporters, Wasn't nobody going to come unless they wanted the whole room to stand up when the priest asked if there was anybody that wanted to object this marriage.

First of all, Sunset had mostly male cousins on both sides of her family so there wasn't any females for her to hang around, and the ones that there were was doing their own thing, and only came out their igloo once a year. Meaning they stayed far away from the family and gossip as possible. As far as aunties and uncles go they never treated Sunset like blood, but more like a regular citizen.

Even friends treat their friends better than her own family treated her. They didn't call her and wish her happy birthday nor could she even get a balloon and a card. They never got her nothing for Christmas or invited her to any family functions so she said to hell with them. She was the youngest to a sister and a brother, but her siblings were thousands and thousands of miles away so what could they possibly do. It wasn't like she kept in touch with them anyway; she didn't even own their number. Sunset's daddy was definitely not going to come, but her mother on the other hand just might make an appearance. Maybe if Sunset wasn't so stubborn and cagey, somebody would've been there for her, but now the only person she had to blame for her current situation was herself.

-

Sunset's mother was watching her soaps in the kitchen when she started feeling a lot of abdominal pain like she felt when she was in labor. She knew one of her kids was in trouble and she knew the good Lord would point the way. Quickly, she grabbed her purse, turned off the TV, and just got in her car letting the Lord be her compass. She ended up at St. Joseph Mercy Hospital where Sunset was. Seeing as though Sunset was the only child that was still here in Michigan, she knew it was Sunset. Sunset's mother Star parked, walked in the entrance, and started talking to the receptionist so she could get Sunset's room number. The elevator going up couldn't have come any faster, but soon as Star hit the third floor she followed the numbers on the wall until she found herself standing right across from Sunset's hospital room. Here it is, Sunset hadn't seen her mother or spoken to her since she was 17, which was the day she moved out to go live with Max.

-

Max refused to come even though Halo had some dope head. He wanted to be rock hard when he knocked the bottom out of her coosie. Parking in front of his garage, he got out of the car and ran to the passenger door trying to open up the door for Halo and be a gentleman for once. As they were sauntering to the front door a piece of paper fell out of Max's back pocket, but his mind was too anticipated on sex to know that Halo bent down in her tracks, and picked up the mysterious piece of paper. Opening up the paper Halo read "the name Sunset, a hospital address, and a telephone number."

"What is this?"

"I know you know what paper looks like don't you. Give it here and bring your ass!" Max commanded looking at Halo's raised hand and the wiggling piece of paper.

"Not this time, I ain't going to bring my ass nowhere."

"I'm only going to ask you once."

"And I'm only going to give you one chance to answer my question!"

"Sunset is my wife." The word wife struck every part of Halo's body like lightning. All this time she was sleeping around with a married man. A man could leave his girlfriend in less than a minute, but in order for a man to leave his wife, that was a more time-consuming departure. Halo knew it was no place for her anymore.

"And she's in the hospital for who knows what going through who knows what with who knows you while you creeping around with me? Hell no! I ain't going nowhere with you son of a bitch! I wonder what else you've been lying to me about. Shame on me to think we had a future!" Halo started punching Max on the head with her Nicole Lee bag so he just threw her over his shoulders and shut the door until he reached the game room. She was still kicking and yelling the whole time, but she must've liked it because if she really wanted to get away she would've got away until she was thrown on top of his pool table. When he threw her on the table, he jammed her head real hard on the corner pocket so she just sat there with her eyes open very statue like while he tore off her shorts, yanked her top off, and beat away at her stillmatic walls.

Sunset was eight centimeters and her mother was right there by her side. Sunset couldn't believe it when she saw her mother. She didn't understand that mothers were like diamonds and guardian angels. And no matter what she did even if she committed a capital crime, her mother was always going to be there for her. Of course it was a bad time to talk so Star just did everything a mother could do for their child while they were in labor. Star couldn't believe Max was absent from this moment, but she knew he was useless all along.

Max was inching his way into Halo's forbidden fruit. Sunset was nine centimeters. Max was pounding Halo so hard you could hear his balls rubbing against the pool table and you could hear his thrusts.

Sunset was ten centimeters and now the doctors were making her push. The first push wasn't quite it. Max was still pushing his limits with Halo steady pushing her walls apart and then he came. He pulled his bare throbber out and let come fall all over Halo's shirt and some come had made its way inside of Halo.

Sunset's second push was quite successful. The head was now outside in the world, and on the third push came out the rest of Sunset's little boy's body.

Out of nowhere Tatum handed Infiniti a long white envelope that was rather bulky. He and Infiniti were sipping on some ocean blue mixed drinks with Malibu Rum, Midon pineapple juice, Sprite, and some other fusions. Infiniti was wondering if she should tell Tatum, Tame was probably on to them, but she decided to keep it to herself. Inching closer to him to give Tatum a hug, Infiniti was dying to let her freaky side takeover just eye-gripping him. After the hug, she started rubbing on his leg more and more to it begin to jump. Tatum didn't know what to do.

"What you doing girl?"

"Something we should've been done a long time ago." After that comment Infiniti's hands were invading their way inside of Tatum pants where his throbber was still hiding.

"We can't do this right now especially not right here."

"Why not, I don't care if you don't care." After one caress of the head, Infiniti felt blessed because she felt Tatum's trophy and finally she was stunned by its measurements and she wanted him to take refuge inside of her.

"Infiniti I have to work," Tatum tried to refuse even though this huge erection bulging in the air wasn't going anywhere until he solved it, and he wanted to give into Infiniti so bad.

"You and I both know you ain't goin be late for work. But as for me, this is an opportunity I know you don't want to refuse." Infiniti took Tatum's ring hand and started rubbing it across her kitty's lips. Tatum figured he mine as well get in between Infiniti's legs. What was the point of him cashing her out if he wasn't banging her? It wasn't like Tame was giving anything up or going to give up anything anytime soon. In Tame's defense she wasn't being her wifely self because she knew Tatum was creeping and sleeping around. Until his creeping was over, she wasn't giving up no pleasure or paradise.

There was no such thing as being half of a cheater or sort of a cheater anyway so if he was going to be a cheater, he mines as well be a full fledge cheater. Tatum convinced himself this was the right thing to do. And since it has been so long since he's gotten any he wanted some quick and fast.

"Check please!" Tatum motioned for their waiter. He left a fat tip by the salt shaker on their table and him and Infiniti rushed to the backseats of his Tange. They entered through the back doors and he let the seats down leaving them more than enough room to boom. Infiniti was about to help Tatum take off her shorts, but he stopped her before she could unbutton them. Infiniti loved this side of Tatum, he had been securing up under a shell so she let Tatum do his thing. He yanked Infiniti's shorts off and let her thong drop to her heels and threw both pieces to the front. Then Tatum took off his forces and climbed out of his boxers along with his pants. He was on his knees and let Infiniti fall back like his seats with her legs spread far apart like an eagle's wings on his shoulders while he gave her the business. He was still a pro despite being so sexually desolate. Good cutty make you come quick, but he didn't. They were in the parking lot for about an hour and half with no intermission before they finally stopped fogging up the Bahama Breeze's parking lot. Infiniti was pleased to finally have gotten Tatum to give it up and was even more pleased that his sex game was a fifty on a scale from 1-10.

69

"Damn we got to do this again," Infiniti broke the silence.

"Yeah we do. I don't even know what I was holding back for."

"Tell me about it." Both Infiniti and Tatum put on the rest of their clothes and climbed into the front seat where he took off so he could drop Infiniti back off at her place and he could serve some law and justice. The sweat that was on their bodies and the smell of sex in the air didn't bother them. Tatum felt three times better than before and he wasn't worried about changing his clothes. If he smelled like another woman when he got home, or even worst sex, then he just did. Infiniti on the other hand was about to wash Tatum off real quick soon as she got in the house just because her day was nowhere near over. If she was going to smell like anything it was going to be bath soap and perfume.

Chapter 7: Surprise, Surprise

Halo was so zoned and wacked out, Max had to pick her up off the table. He shot upstairs, washed up, put on some fresh clothes, grabbed a shirt out of Sunset's closet, and gave it to Halo to put on. All she did was clench it in her hand. Halo knew it was time to go so she just walked herself out of the house and sat in the car without following Max around. She was still feeling woozy, but she had enough of Max, and she knew Tame was right. She missed Harlan like hell. She had never been treated like such filth before. Never had a man showed her such disrespect or had she met a man with zero respect for his house or himself.

Max figured he mine as well give Halo alimony for the shit he had been putting her through. He gave Halo a stack of 100 dollar bills before she exited the silent ride, but that still didn't make Halo talk. Halo just made sure Max had his piece of paper, pocketed the money, and took shelter back in the guestroom hoping Tame wouldn't bother her.

Max started pushing it towards the hospital, but it was too late. His almost five pound baby boy was born and in his mother's arms after Star held him and prayed over his life. Sunset wanted to name the baby after his daddy, but since he had broken her heart beyond belief she was trying to think of a better name as she admired her seed that resembled both of his parents.

-

When Infiniti got out of the shower, she started counting her money until her phone started ringing. *I wonder who this is.*

"Hello."

71

"Hey Infiniti this is Tier."

"Oh yeah what's up?"

"You think we can get better acquainted today?"

"For show, just come to my house at 7452 Pinewood Trail."

"I heard of that street. I stay in West Bloomfield too in a studio apartment," Tier lied. It wasn't no damn studio apartments in West Bloomfield. It wasn't nothing, but land, businesses, and big houses. Tier lived in a big house by herself that was paid for by her hustler methods too and she had a maid. Infiniti didn't have a maid, but not because she couldn't afford one. A maid was an expense that she could spare.

"I guess you can find it on your own then. Well I'll see you shortly." Infiniti was just sitting in the living room watching music videos on her Smart TV when she heard somebody's loud bass coming closer and closer to her house. Peeking through her silk curtains, Infiniti saw who she distinguished as Tier driving an 2014 RL Acura to be exact which made Infiniti wonder what the hell Tier did for a living, or if she had a rich, wealthy family. Infiniti's whole perspective of Tier was beginning to alter like an ego. She knew rich people could be suckers, but that was only some of them. The rich were too damn cocky to let anybody run over them. It seems Infiniti was going to have to start asking her little diamond in the rough more questions.

"Nice car, surprise you ain't gone deaf by now as cranked up as your music was," Infiniti greeted Tier at the door.

"Please tell me I'm not dreaming and this is your house," Tier let herself in like her house wasn't just as marvelous.

"This is all me right here and I'm going to need you to take off your shoes."

"Don't you need a roommate or want a roommate?" Tier rubbed in like she was homeless and dying to get a piece of Infiniti's capital.

"No I don't so why did you move up here out of all the places you could move too?"

"I was just tired of being down south and this is a good northern city at least in the history books it is."

"I guess do you stay by yourself? You met that scourge you called a boyfriend up here or what?"

"Yeah I stay by myself and yeah I met him up here."

"So driving a car like that you must have a job or somebody paying your bills why you trying to front like you a loner and lonely?" Lucky for Tier Infiniti's phone started ringing and she took it in another room.

"Hello."

"Hey there," Infiniti realized it was Gunz from the other night.

"Oh hi."

"I know we ain't really hit it off like dat yet, but I need you to do me a favor if you will."

"Talk to me Gunz baby."

"I want you to find out some info for me and I promise to make it worth your while on dat money tip. After we get off the phone you can come get mi down payment."

"I'm down."

"Mi girl Chariot told me she was an RN at a hospital. She had the hospital clothes, badge, and everything, but I got ear-sey she's a skank trying to trick me."

"Say no more I got you tonight boo."

"My address is 2095 Cliffside Drive in Wixom."

"I'll be there and if you don't mind I'll have a guest with me, but disregard that because she'll stay in the car."

"It's cool my queen." Walking out of the library, Infiniti tiptoed up to where Tier was last seen to make sure she didn't have a thief on her hands and she didn't.

"I just want you to know you're rolling with me today."

"Fine with me."

"Well I'm about to put on something explicit so I'll see you in a minute. The kitchen is through those doors over there and the remote is on the coffee table." While Infiniti was upstairs Tier couldn't stop thinking. She knew she was going to have to keep a bunch of lies going to stay on Infiniti's team so she wouldn't catch on. And she couldn't wait to go out and fill up her phonebook.

"Alright thanks." Seeing that Infiniti had millions of clothes, she could afford to change her clothes a million times. Infiniti had to dress for the occasion, and she refused to let another man see her in the same outfit one man saw her in. That was like sleeping with somebody in dirty sheets. It was side jobs like these that kept bread in Infiniti's pockets because her house and her cars were paid for. The only thing Infiniti had to pay was utility bills which was nothing, but chump change. Infiniti was always stashing 50% of her deviant money in her savings and blowing the other 50%. Infiniti guessed a dress would do the trick for confronting a lying girlfriend and enticing a newbie. Infiniti came out with a short backless dress, the matching stilettos and accessories. Infiniti had flat-ironed her hair bone straight and accented her outfit with a dressy hat.

-

Once Max reached Sunset's room, the baby was in the nursery, and Star and Sunset was catching up. Star could've been rubbing the situation all up in Sunset's face especially after noticing the rock she had stationed on her ring finger, but she wasn't that type of mother. Instead her concerns were more about the baby because she didn't want to push her daughter away anymore. Max was shocked to see Star there. He almost dropped the gifts he was bearing. He had a bouquet of roses with a teddy bear, balloons, and a diaper bag with their son's go home outfit in it and a new outfit for Sunset to go home in. When Star and Sunset saw the gifts they softened up the fire in their eyes.

"I don't know if I can forgive you for missing the birth of your first seed."

"I'm here now," Max walked in.

"You were barely there during my pregnancy, not to mention I went into preterm labor and anything could've happened to me or our baby and you would've never known." Max was just waiting for Star to put her two cents in, but to his surprise she exited the room. She hoped her daughter wouldn't be a stranger anymore and wouldn't leave her grandson out of her life, but the only way for her to know that was to leave. It wasn't much she could do being there while they argued anyway.

"I really am sorry."

"I know you're sorry. What was so important you couldn't be with me?" Can you tell me that? Matter fact I could care less, but I'm about to call the nurse in so that you can see the baby while you're still here. You can go sign the birth certificate, and we can give this baby a name."

"What happened to Max Jr?"

"Hell no! You're already my baby's father and my husband. That's enough right there."

"Well can he at least have my middle name?"

"I guess." When the nurse brought the baby in Max's face lit up and he felt kind of bad he missed the birth of his son who was so identical to him. Max became attached at the sight of him and picked him up.

"Let's name him Samell Jonah Lee."

"Okay." After Sunset fed the baby she went to sleep while the baby and Max bonded until it was time for Samell to go back to the nursery. She thought her mother just went to the vending machine or something, but she figured she went home. She was just thankful for her mother's presence period so she took that in consideration. She didn't want to think about when they were going to finally patch up their relationship in the future even though she needed to. Clearly patching up her relationship with her husband wasn't going to get her anywhere, but sad and lonely.

-

When Tier saw Infiniti she could see she had expensive taste too, and hoped Infiniti was done with the questions.

"Follow me were leaving out the garage."

"You driving?"

"That would make sense wouldn't it? I mean I don't know how long you've been up here, but I'm pretty sure you ain't learned your way around that swiftly. Not to mention I don't need no chauffeur while I do my missions."

"Yeah you right." Infiniti opted to drive her LR2, raisin black 15' Range Rover. Tier wondered how many other cars Infiniti owned. Pulling out the garage, Infiniti cranked up her music too. It took about thirty minutes for Infiniti to get to Gunz' palace. Once Infiniti reached the gate, she spoke to Gunz' security guard who wasn't there last time she was over.

"Yes I'm here to see Gunz."

"Your name is?"

"Infiniti."

"Go ahead and drive right in. He's expecting you." Driving in, Infiniti almost smacked the black out of Tier who was acting like she was in a dream world again."

"Will you please close your mouth and stick your eyeballs back in your head."

"Sorry damn, but this house is ten times better than your house."

"Yeah it's nice, but you better get some self-control. Maybe you ain't use to living large, but I am and I'll be right back."

"Why can't I go?"

"Oh no sweetie, I don't bring nobody around the dudes I mess with especially not no girl scout in training." That was a smart move for Infiniti because Tier was indeed the type of female who would f her best friend's man behind their back, but she just let it go and sat in the car. Infiniti held her purse in front of her and waited for someone to come to the door after she rang the doorbell. Gunz came to the door a few seconds later or less.

"You look more beautiful then you looked the first day I saw you mi queen."

"Thank you I thought you would like this number."

"Well everything you need is in this duffel bag so we'll hook up later tonight."

"Alright I'll see you then." Strolling out Infiniti carried her duffel bag to the trunk and could only imagine what Tier was thinking. She probably thought Infiniti was selling drugs, but she wasn't responsive when Infiniti got in the driver's seat so Infiniti just headed to her next place of business.

Chapter 8: Trap Day

Finally Halo arose from the state of shock she was in reminiscing on the last event that took place in her shirt. She wondered why a shirt she didn't recognize was laying in her bed. Still she pulled the ejaculated filled shirt over her head hastily and ran to the shower like it was a portal. Once Halo got fully dressed and comfy she searched the house for Tame so they could talk. Halo realized the house was empty and she was the only person there. On Halo's wild search for her long lost sister she couldn't take her pupils off of this peculiar China cabinet in the living room. It was bad enough Tame's house was decorated like it was 1952, but Tame was a voodoo doll collector?

Tame had a dozen voodoo dolls in the cabinet with needles pressed through them she had collected from her and Tatum's out of country trips. Halo hoped that her sister didn't use dolls to seek vengeance against people which she didn't, but she did name one of her dolls Infiniti. If only Tame knew what kind of witchcraft she was indulging in. The doll specified for Infiniti would probably have pins in it and anything else necessary to make her suffer. Halo hoped her sister wasn't heading for the mountain cliffs of insanity.

Halo wondered where could Tame sneak off too since she didn't like the outside world. The only reason why Tame had been having some discrepancies with the way things had been going down lately was because Tatum was out cheating while she was at home slaving to keep the house clean and being a lingerie and stripper clothes designer. Her clothing line Popsicle was her everything so she didn't really care to do anything else except get to the bottom of the big hole in her relationship. Tatum was a good man prior to Infiniti's arrival in his life. Infiniti was a different breed of woman though and that is how she managed to turn a good man bad, but Tame wasn't going down like that. Nor did she want the satisfaction of pleasure. She just wanted her husband back. Her definition and interpretation of marriage didn't compare to anybody else's. That's why she was the wifey and even after a man makes mistakes she was still going to be wifey.

-

Tame was headed for the Manhattan Club so she could drop off this month's wardrobe, then service De Ja Vu Detroit, and later she was going to make her last delivery to De Ja Vu Flint. Carmella was the first person to discover Tame's fashion design expertise. Tame had been running an ad on Craiglist for the longest. She had called around to many strip clubs before Carmella answered her prayers and got her hooked up with De Ja Vu. Usually, Tame would get the doormen to get the shipment and leave, but today she decided to go inside and get a drink after the doormen carried the shipment to the dressing room.

"Hi Dakota," Tame greeted seating herself at the bar.

"Carmella got you working the bar today?"

"No, but you know I can fix you something."

"Let me get an Incredible Hulk."

"I didn't know you were a drinker."

"I drink occasionally, but how's Cardi doing?"

"I got my eyes on him right now," Dakota claimed making Tame's drink.

"Girl let me tell you the other day he was having a wet dream right…"

"So what's wrong with that?"

"He kept saying this hoe named **Infiniti** so I poured some frozen water on his ass," Dakota laughed adding the last ingredient to Tame's drink.

"I hope you're not a victim of Infiniti too." If only Dakota knew Infiniti wasn't the only female she should be worried about.

"Is Tatum fooling around with a hoe named Infiniti too?" Dakota asked sliding Tame her drink across the bar knowing her bartending skills wouldn't fail her and she wouldn't have to make Tame another drink because she made it strong.

"Yeah."

"So what are you going to do?" Tame gobbled the drink down before answering.

"I don't know about you, but I'm going to make Infiniti's life a living hell," or so she thought. After that comment Tame grabbed her purse and left for stop number three.

-

The only reason Dakota was at the bar so early was because Carmella asked Dakota to come in and work with some of the strippers she just hired. She knew this was the perfect opportunity to get some alone time with her bae. Since Cardi wasn't coming to her she knew she was going to have to go to Cardi so she drove to her niece's townhouse. She saw his car in front of their garage so she knew he was there. Knocking on their door, she rung the doorbell, and waited for him to answer knowing he wouldn't play hard to get. Since Cardi didn't see Dakota on the other side of him, he went to open the door after hearing the doorbell. When he went to the door, he wished he would've stayed in the bed and put the pillows over his ears, or looked out the peephole.

"What are you doing here Carmella?"

"I wanted to see you. Didn't you want to see me?"

"I see you every day at work isn't that enough," Cardi said wiping the sleep out of his eyes.

"No it's not. It's about time we make a trip to the bedroom don't you think?"

"You got me messed up if you think I'm about to knock you off in my bed or in my house."

"What's the matter are you going to tell her? We use to live in the same household all of us, and you was knocking me up, off, and on so what's the problem?" Carmella said getting real close to Cardi even though he had morning breath, slob on his face, and still had sleep in his eyes.

"No, I'm not going to tell her, but I can't keep doing this with you. This shit is wrong."

"Yeah it's wrong and I can always tell her you know."

"No come in so we can get this over with." Cardi snatched Carmella by her hand pulling her in and slamming and locking the door. Carmella didn't look like a 40-year-old hag today even though she wasn't 40. She was really 34, but people just presumed that because she wore those busy old-fashioned hairdos and she had a poor sense of fashion. She looked ten years younger today. Her body was already perfect seeing as though she never had any kids, she didn't have a tall hairstyle on the top of her head, and she had on a banging outfit. She figured Cardi wouldn't be able to keep his hands off of her. It would be different if he had to screw a sloppy, fat, old lady, but Carmella was none of the above. She was still beautiful, stacked, and slim. He led her into the basement, made her take off her jeans so she wouldn't get her coochie liquor all over them, and bent her over the couch since she loved it frombe. Even though she erupted and he had erupted, he couldn't stop himself. He just kept going and going and Carmella didn't bother to stop him because that's exactly what she wanted. She really wanted something else too to seal the deal so she could trap him.

Today was an ovulation holiday for her as a matter of fact. Since Cardi wasn't letting up Carmella decided to take the rest of her clothes off exposing the rest of her bodacious body.

"I'm sorry I haven't been paying you any attention lately. You are glowing today." Cardi claimed when really it was just the sex talking.

"That's okay." Carmella responded as Cardi stripped too knowing she would make him pay later. They embarked on good sex for the next three hours off and on the couch. After they were finished caboodling they talked a little bit, but it was mainly Carmella trying to influence Cardi into going on a weekend getaway to Chicago which wasn't really for vacation reasons.

-

Evening was approaching so Infiniti decided she would drop in on Harlan since he hadn't called her in a couple of days. She wanted to make sure he wasn't stressing off of that crooked angel Halo. Tier was still asleep so Infiniti just let her be knowing she was going to be in and out. Plus she wanted to test Tier once again to see if she could be trusted. Infiniti left her keys and her duffle bag in arm's reach. Infiniti fixed her dress as she rang Harlan's doorbell.

For the last couple of days Harlan had been thinking a lot about Infiniti and now look where she was. Harlan practically jumped down the stairs to let Infiniti in. Infiniti couldn't believe Harlan had on some boxers and some pajama pants which were sagging.

"Please don't tell me you've been cooped up in the house?" Harlan pulled Infiniti in and hugged her.

"I missed you," Harlan sighed, but Infiniti didn't return the phrase.

"I'm pretty sure you did, but I was just in the neighborhood and thought I would stop by."

"So am I going to see you more?" Harlan asked sitting on the sofa while Infiniti sat on the arm of his sofa knowing exactly where Harlan was going.

"Look Harlan I enjoy the time we spend together, but as I have said before I'm not ready for a relationship, and you shouldn't be ready for a new relationship either. I don't know how fast you heal, but I know you haven't healed yet because you just broke up with Halo a couple days ago. I will tell you this, when I do settle down I hope that I can do it with you." Infiniti could tell that wasn't what Harlan wanted to hear, but she wasn't about to plant no lies in his mind.

"Come on cheer up you look like you lost your best friend."

"Well I need to get back to work so I think you better go." Infiniti was shocked by Harlan's attitude, but she respected his wishes and left. *I was about to leave anyway.*

Tier was still a sleeping beauty when Infiniti hopped back in the truck, but soon as Infiniti turned up the volume Tier began to stretch. Infiniti figured she was going to stop messing with Harlan like that and was on her way to the nearest BP so she could gas up, check her duffle bag, and hit the road.

-

Back at the Manhattan Club, Dakota had her hands full with the three new strippers whose names were Purple, Fantasy, and Lola. Purple had her hair in some underhand braids that was jet black with purple streaks, and she was offbeat. Lola was the fastest learner, and Fantasy just kept pulling out her mirror, and twiddling with her light brown hair every time they start dancing.

"Why aren't you a stripper?" Purple asked.

"Because my boyfriend wouldn't be with me if I was one."

"What's your boyfriend name, I bet I could turn him out," Lola gave Fantasy a hi-five. All of a suddenly an idea popped in Dakota's mind.

"Is that so?" Dakota asked, but Lola wondered if she should've kept that joke to herself, but she was just being real.

"Sure can, not many men can refuse these tongue and seductive skills."

"On the real, I think my boyfriend's cheating and since you can turn my man out, why don't you get him to sleep with you so I can turn him loose."

"Don't worry about it let me meet him and I'll bring it back to you on DVD."

"Okay if I can teach you some more tricks, I can probably have you on stage tonight, and you'll meet him, he's one of the DJ's."

"I know exactly who you talking about. I saw him the day I auditioned. You got a deal." Dakota and Lola were as serious as an eviction notice. Speaking of Cardi, Dakota wondered why Patrick was on the turntables since he was the backup DJ. Cardi could've rode with Dakota so she went to go have a little chat with Pat.

"Hey Pat how come you on the tables today?"

"Carmella told me Cardi wasn't feeling good and had a little virus."

"A virus? What kind of virus? He wasn't sick when I left the house earlier."

"Well I don't know what to tell you that's just what she told me." Dakota was deep in suspicion about Cardi and her aunt. Did they have something freaky going on? She figured her mind was just playing tricks on her so she got back to the dancing, and got to know the girls a little better especially Lola."

-

The doctors estimated Samell wasn't going to be coming home for about two weeks. They wanted to make sure he gained some more weight, but overall he was healthy as he could be. Sunset was still furious with Max, but she had Tame's determination. Every since Sunset got released from the hospital, Max has been at her side shockingly. He was scared he was going to find Star hanging around the house which he didn't want, but everything Star said would happen did and she knew that Sunset would leave him. Of course he wasn't going to get off that easily, but if he wanted to remain married, and if he wanted to be a father to his newborn son it was sacrifices he was going to have to make. Sunset called herself making a deal with Max, but she was more so forcing his hand. He obviously didn't want to give up his youth, but he expected Sunset to give up hers?

Whether Max wanted to believe it or not, he was 29, married, and now he had a child he had to support, and be a role model too unless he wanted to live life with his child and his child's mother hating him for the rest of his life. Besides, now that Sunset dropped her baby, her nest would be up and running in no time so Max's need for Halo was no longer necessary so he planned to tell Sunset everything. He was going to break it off with Halo forever, little did he know Halo was long past done with him.

-

Infiniti told Tier to go inside the gas station, pay for the gas, and get her something to munch on purposely so she could check out her duffle bag in peace. Once Infiniti saw that Tier was inside the gas station Infiniti popped the trunk and unzipped the bag. Enclosed was ten stacks, a digital camera, directions, and pictures of Chariot who had brown autumn skin, Tabasco red hair, wore fake eyelashes, waxed eyebrows, an eyebrow ring, training bra titties, a white girl stomach, thunder thighs, and so forth. Infiniti couldn't wait to catch Chariot dirty dancing, and began smiling devilishly. She hurried up, zipped her bag back up, secured it close to her seat, and closed the trunk back while pumping her 87 unleaded gas. Infiniti was right on time because Tier was coming out of the gas station and couldn't wait to see where they were headed this time now that she was alert.

"You sure you don't want nothing because we got a long ride ahead of us. We're going to a strip club tonight which means drinking, which means you better know your limits. You better know how to control your liquor because I'll leave you at the bar if you make an ass out of yourself," Infiniti said as she put the pump back on its post, closed her gas cap, and drove off.

Chapter 9: Stripper Units

Just as Lola and Dakota agreed they were going to take Cardi down, and tonight was going to be the night. Dakota had taught Lola the basics so she could start twirling on the pole, but Lola came out the woodwork with her own pole tricks. Instantly, Dakota knew Lola was bout that stripper life.

Dakota never thought that stripping was going to be so damn entertaining, meaning she could break or make or a relationship, but it was.

Cardi was on his way to work so he could take over the turntables and Carmella was at home resting crossing her fingers, dotting her t's, and positive she was pregnant while Lola prepared for her first appearance on stage. Lola was in the dressing room getting to know some of the other strippers that worked there, and digging the stripper apparel they could choose from. Remembering a talk Dakota had with Tamale and Spicy, she pulled Lola to the side once again.

"Please don't tell anybody about this. I believe some of the other strippers that work here have tried to talk to Cardi, but he didn't budge so maybe we'll get him drunk a little bit. And I know he'll probably be looking out for me so I'll make sure I stay out the way."

"Don't worry I got this," Lola assured her. Dakota wondered if she was out of her mind or if she was really going to get the closure she wanted by giving another girl permission to record herself getting down and dirty with her man or if she was just being paranoid.

-

With the help of Infiniti's GPS system, Tier and her reached De Ja Vu in Flint right around the same time Tame did, which happened to be accurate with the sun setting and all the freaks coming out or in other words, strippers. While Tame was getting the doormen to come get the boxes out her car, Infiniti was getting out of her truck, and opening up the duffel bag so she could retrieve her digital camera right quick and get ready to take down Chariot. Usually, Tame would be headed to the highway since she had a long way, but her body was calling for some intoxicants so she went inside to the bar while Infiniti and Tier sat down at a table.

"So Tier how many sex partners have you had?" Infiniti questioned to find out how experienced Tier was sexually.

"Is that supposed to be a trick question?" Tier played dumb yet again just because she was really trying to play Infiniti, and honestly she had lost a long time ago.

"You can lie if you want to, but that want benefit you one bit and for the record I don't ask trick questions."

While they were talking, Tame ordered a Dirty Mexican Lemonade.

"Three."

"And how would you rate them on a scale from one to ten?"

"I can't compare them to a number." Infiniti reached in her purse and grabbed a twenty dollar bill.

"Will you please get me a Kamikaze and get yourself something too."

"Sure." Tier got up and walked over to the bar. She stood right on the side of Tame. *That girl Tier is something else, but I know that liquor a get her talking.* As Tier was standing at the bar she couldn't remember what drink Infiniti wanted because she started thinking about some other shit. All she knew was it started with a K and didn't want to risk Infiniti dogging her out or trying too so she asked Tame.

"Excuse me do you know what mixed drink starts with the letter K"?

"A Kamikaze."

"Yeah that's it, thank you so much." Tier really didn't want to embarrass herself anymore since she really wasn't a drinker, so she just got what Infiniti got and hoped she was going to like it.

"Can I get 2 Kamikazes?"

"Two Kamikazes coming up."

"You work here?" Tame asked trying to figure out Tier a little bit. She figured she was either under 21 or a lesbian since her appearance made her look younger then what she really was, and she was at a female strip club, but let Tier's ID state it she was 20.

"Oh no, I'm here with my friend Infiniti." At the time, Tame was about to swallow her drink, but once she heard Infiniti's name in the air again she spit alcohol all over the bar top. And really couldn't imagine what the hell Infiniti would be doing at a female strip club. She hoped Infiniti wasn't bisexual.

"Do you know her or something?" Tier asked trying to figure out why Tame discharged her drink from her mouth.

"You can say that," Tame lied figuring she could probably get some valuable information out of Tier.

"Have you ridden in her pretty little G6 yet?"

"No, but I did ride in her Range Rover and I've been to her house. I still can't believe how amazing she's living, "Tier bragged. Infiniti looked over at the bar to see if Tier was still there which she was and noticed she was talking to somebody that looked familiar. *I wonder who she's talking too because I can't see her knowing anybody all the way out here.*

"Are y'all related or something?"

"No, were just friends. I just moved up here and she told me she'll show me the ropes."

"Oh, really," Tame could just imagine what ropes Infiniti was going to show her.

"Well it was nice vibing with you, but I got to go," Tier grabbed the drinks and dipped.

"Wait, here's my card. My number is on the back. Maybe we can hang out sometime."

"Oh sure." As Tier was going back to the table, Tame downed her drink and left before she blew her cover.

"Who the hell were you lolli-gagging with?"

"Oh, some lady she was real friendly. She said she knew you actually." Infiniti thought to herself for a moment. *I don't have no relatives in Flint and the last time I had a female friend was high school so who is this bitch?"*

"Did she tell you her name?"

"No, oh yeah she gave me a business card." Tier flipped the card over so she could fill Infiniti's curiosity.

"Tame." Infiniti couldn't believe it. *I guess that bitch is really out to get me. I'm going to have to handle her.*

De Ja Vu Showgirls had a full house and all the strippers were starting to surface. Infiniti saw a girl with Chariot's descriptions at the bar seconds later.

"Jackpot, there goes our girl." Infiniti spoke out of the blue even though Tier didn't have a clue what the hell Infiniti was ranting about. And she was focusing in on a dude who was sitting at a bar, and another who was tipping a stripper, and another who was just entering.

Chariot got her regular drink which was a Panty Dropper like always before she went on stage because she hated stripping, but the boss threatened to kill her if she quit and she wanted her own money in case her and Gunz didn't work out so she did what she had to do. Infiniti snapped pictures of Chariot doing it all; sliding down the pole, giving various males lap dances, the whole nine yards. Nobody said anything to Infiniti either about her snapping pictures inside the strip club because everybody was too busy focusing in on the titties and asses on stage.

Chariot's stripper name was Hot Sauce and she wasn't a bad stripper, but she was a lonely stripper now that Infiniti had substantial verification. Even though, Infiniti's job was done she wasn't about to leave without rubbing it in Chariot's face, or without Tier who had abandoned the table so Infiniti bought Chariot a Bacardi Orgasm and gave the bartender orders to send her to Infiniti's table whenever she came and got the shot.

Tier went and sat by the dude who was funding a stripper. She actually snatched one of his dollar bills out of his hand and put it in her bra.

"That wasn't meant for you unless you a stripper too."

"I don't work here, but I could be your personal stripper if you let me."

"Say no more you should call me tonight so we can hook something up."

"Okay what you waiting for? Give me your number." Tier handed the fine gentleman her phone so he could personally make himself a contact in her phonebook.

"What's your name boo?"

"It's Sal."

"Well Sal if you goin be messing with me you goin have to chill out with the whole strip club scene." Sal was about to be out of dollars anyway so he got up and left which was good for Tier so he wouldn't see her flirting with any of the other men she was about to flirt with. She still had a little bit of time before Infiniti would be on her trail so she bounced to the bar for number two where this handsome, breath-taking, guy was sitting conversing with the bartender.

"Come on baby you and I both know you can do better than a bartender at a strip joint," Tier whispered in his ear which cut his conversation short.

"And by that I guess you mean yourself?"

"Yeah you're catching on."

"Well what are you doing here then?"

"I'm a conspirator in business unlike you."

"How you know I'm not doing business either?"

"Well maybe you are, but I saw you sitting over here, and I didn't want to leave here without you giving me your number."

"And what makes you think I'm just going to give you my number?"

"Because deep inside you and I both know you want too. You rather try your luck with a bartender; somebody who sees men and women every day? Ain't no telling what type of woman she is."

"You got a point." Again Tier slid her phone into his hands and asked for his name for her memory bank.

"I didn't catch your name?"

"That's because you didn't ask, but its Owen."

"Alright now, I'll be talking too you later." Soon as Tier turned her back to see what Infiniti was doing they made eye contact. Just when she was getting started, she hoped she was still in the clear which she was.

"Chariot you've got a drink and an invitation to Table 10," the bartender explained. In Chariot's head she thought it was a man who bought her the drink, but it wasn't. She had drunk her shot and sat the empty shot glass at an empty table before she got to Table 10. When Chariot reached Table 10 she was surprised to see two females since no female have made advances at her before, but at least the two females sitting in front of her were bad compared to the old, fat, bald-headed men she was use to.

Infiniti scooted her chair out and tapped her lap.

"What I got money too; ain't you goin give me a lap dance?" Chariot couldn't believe she was about to give a female a lap dance and Tier couldn't believe Infiniti was about to pay for a lap dance from a female. Soon as Chariot tooted her ass up in the air and was about to start dancing for the dollars, Infiniti burst out laughing and pushed Chariot away from her.

"Bitch I was just playing. I don't want no lap dance from you, but I do want to let you know you're busted! Tier exhaled in relief that Infiniti wasn't a lesbian at least she hoped she wasn't because Tier wanted penis in her life, and didn't want to risk being turned out or learning any lessons female wise.

"What you mean I'm busted?

"You thought he wasn't going to find out you was a stripper because you come all the way out here to dip it low?" Chariot realized exactly what was going on.

"Oh, don't worry I promise you I'll take care of Gunz for you. As a matter of fact, I'm about to go lay and play with him right now," Infiniti got up and Tier tailed behind her.

Chariot reached for Infiniti's arm, "please don't tell him, I'll pay you. I'll do whatever you want, but please don't tell him."

"Let me go, I don't have no sympathy for you and you ain't got enough money to pay me. My dress costs more than your daily salary." Chariot just stood there looking confounded as Infiniti and Tier split.

-

Almost home, Tame pondered about a million things she could've done to Infiniti, she wanted to do to Infiniti, and was going to do to Infiniti, but deep inside she knew it would've been bad timing so she sucked that shit up and went in the house. Tame couldn't believe Tatum was there, but she was happy she knew Infiniti's location because they obviously weren't going to see each other tonight. And she remembered Halo was there so she hurried up and unlocked the door to make sure Tatum didn't stab her heart once again, but he was sleep in the bedroom which was shocking too since he barely ever went to sleep. Halo was still sleep in the guest room which was even more shocking because lately all she's been doing is sleeping. Tame never knew sleep was so damn interesting.

-

Cardi saw that there were three new strippers there when he arrived at his turntables. He was astonished he didn't see Dakota nowhere around. It was a note left on his DJ equipment to announce the three new strippers. Since he wanted to be nosy, he went over to the new faces so he could meet them firsthand since they were stationed at the bar.

"Hi, y'all doing ladies, my name is Cardi and I'm the DJ most of the time and I just wanted to formally introduce myself."

"My name is Purple," Purple twirled her black and purple braids a little bit around her fingers.

"I guess they call you Purple because of them little purple streaks you got?"

"Yep."

"My name is Fantasy as in I got a lot of fantasies and I could make your fantasies come true."

"Okay I got that, and what's your name sweetie?" Cardi asked pointing towards Lola.

"Oh, don't you want to know."

"I sure do."

"They call me Lola make sure you don't forget it."

"I won't," Cardi started eye-balling Lola. She kind of reminded him of Infiniti a little bit with the way she talked. Not to mention she had that hourglass body. Cardi knew better to cross the stripper lines, but he had to get a hit of this one. He was wondering if Lola was lusting over him the same way.

"Well I guess I got to do the DJ thing."

"I'm trying to do some other things," Lola didn't bother to whisper. From that moment on Cardi knew Lola wanted him too. The only question was when and where because with Dakota around he would only get one chance. He was already in enough trouble, but looks like he wanted more.

-

Infiniti ditched Tier and went off to Gunz' house to present him with the goods he had requested and dip and dabble with him like she said she was. Following the gate process again, Gunz met Infiniti at the door.

"Hi queen."

"Hi," Infiniti showed Gunz the pictures and after he reviewed them he broke the camera.

"I knew it!"

"Why you tripping then just X her out of your life."

"You right queen. " Infiniti slipped out of her dress instantly and pulled down Gunz' pants.

"You want this V or what?"

"Hell yeah."

"Come get it then," Infiniti took off running not knowing where the hell she was going and Gunz took off after her. Infiniti went up some stairs, hit some corners, and ended up in the master bedroom which was the jackpot for her.

-

Leaving work in urgency, Chariot hoped she still had a boyfriend and she still lived with him. Infiniti fell into their bed and Gunz fell on top of her done chasing, ready to relinquish some of his anger and frustration, but it was no biggie to Infiniti. She couldn't always be the leader in the bedroom. Infiniti moaned extra loud just in case Chariot was on her way home which she knew she was, and Gunz was trying to wear Infiniti's V out the way he was breaking Infiniti's water line over and over again. Chariot wondered if Gunz had told the guard anything, but all she could do was try, but since the guard didn't act strange, she parked her car, and opened the door. Infiniti begged Gunz to stop while Chariot walked up the stairs. Gunz held Infiniti's legs in his arms missionary while he continued busting her insides open.

"Wait," Infiniti interrupted wanting to relocate. As she got up there was that face that she wanted to see.

Chapter 10: Tongue Tied and Twisted

Parlaying with boredom, Tier decided to call Tame wanting to hang out like Tame had claimed they would one day even though they had just met. She wanted to know what Tame wanted with Infiniti. Maybe she could be of some justice. Tame wasn't use to her phone ascending at a late hour so she picked it up hoping it wasn't no hurdle on the other end.

"Hey Tame," Tier screamed like she was high or drunk.

"Who is this?" Tier didn't understand Tame's level of annoyance.

"It's me Tier from the club earlier."

"It hasn't even been 24 hours yet and you already buzzing for me. You must be lonely or desperate."

"I just wanted to hang out with you."

"Hang out why? Hang out where? Is this your number?" Tier was beginning to wonder why Tame was being so offish.

"Yeah, you can reach me at this number."

"Well, I'm straight. I'll holler at you another time another day."

"My bad damn." Tame just hung up and went back to sleep. On that note, Tier decided to call her ex that she was crying about rather pretending to cry about the day she met Infiniti. Behind those fake tears were wishes that he became single overnight. She opted to test the waters and see if he changed his mind. Christion didn't answer Tier's call though nor did he stop his girlfriend Riana from calling right back and giving whoever was going to be on the other end a bitter piece of her mind.

"Pass me your phone," Riana demanded after hearing it sound off. Christion didn't refuse either, he just handed it over like a good boy knowing exactly what was about to happen next.

"Bitch do you know what time it is?" Riana asked soon as Tier answered.

"It's 12:52," Tier answered sarcastically. Riana almost got caught up in Tier's sarcastic humor, but she pulled her authority together.

"I know you know who I am and I know you know that Christion is wide awake laying right here right now and it ain't nothing you can do about it so call back between 9 to 5. Old wham, bam, thank you ma'am, ass hoe." Tier just soaked everything Riana said in.

"I then told you; if you goin screw around, don't screw around with no dumb, disrespectful ass hoes." Riana evaluated getting back in the bed and giving Christion his cellular device back without no beat down or no break-up simply because Riana rather be the main chick then the other woman.

Tier was just checking her luck, but she wasn't even lusting over Christion no more. Reconsidering the two men she met from the tavern earlier, Tier was trying to pick which one she wanted to get turned up with. Any-mini-miney-moe, and the grand prize goes to Owen.

Dialing Owen, Tier almost thought he wasn't going to pick up, but he did.

"What it do?"

"Yeah I wanted to speak to Owen."

"Baby, you ain't never got to worry about nobody else ever answering my phone and I was just wondering how I was going to end my night."

"You better end it with me; by the way my name is Tierney. I don't know what your motif is, but I'm not trying to go catch a movie or just go get a bite. I'm on a whole nother level."

"I got you my baby just give me your address and I'll be there in a jiffy. We can go back to my crib and get it popping."

"I hope you stay by yourself as much as I love a fight."

"I'm not even cut like that." When Tier and Owen joined forces, Tier ended up in West Bloomfield Hills at Owen's house. He had a nice ride, his house was smaller than Gunz' but bigger then Infiniti's, and good energy. After a bit of talking, the two undressed and started sexing like they was listening to an R. Kelly joint until they wore each other out.

-

Cardi had been gawking Lola down all night and he knew that she was directing every dance move she did for him. Cardi hadn't seen Dakota all night, and was flabbergasted when Lola went in for the kill. After she did her solo onstage and wiped every pocket in the building dry, she approached him.

"Stop looking around for your girl boy she ain't here."

"So what you saying?"

"I'm saying what's up between me and you? I know you want to hit this. She will never know because I ain't going to tell. All you got to do is meet me at my place." Cardi licked his lips at the thought of him going up inside of Lola even though he had already worked one body today, he still wanted more like most men do.

Lola was only 19 and had her own place. She was taking care of business. She didn't know how old Cardi really was, nor did she care because she thought she had done it all, and she was a mini Infiniti. She loved her pleasure and she loved working her kitten on a dude's threshold.

"Okay I can do that."

"We'll be closing up soon so when we do, I'll just follow you home."

"You do that," Lola responded exposing her tongue ring and going back to join the other girls. Soon as the club closed up Cardi was right on Lola's bumper. He had a couple of shots of a drink called a Royal Caribbean, but he wasn't drunk. He was completely aware of everything and that he was about to cheat on Dakota with girl number three. Inside the car, Lola phoned Dakota on the way to her apartment.

"Yeah, Dakota everything is going as planned and he's right behind me."

"Okay make sure you take him down for me."

"Don't worry about it, I got you girl." Hanging up Lola whipped into her complex and pulled into her designated parking space. Cardi parked in a guest parking spot. As Lola unlocked the door, she felt the heat rising from Cardi's pants. Cardi wasn't even going to let Lola close the door behind her before he got her skirt down, but Lola made sure her door was locked. She started kissing Cardi passionately as a distraction leading him into her bedroom. She turned the hidden camera on that was hidden behind perfume bottles on her dresser during their kisses, and then the unclothing, and then it was on. Cardi was giving Lola the business.

-

Neither Max nor Sunset could sleep so Sunset kept nudging Max for that big talk.

"So who is she?"

"Come on man can we talk about this tomorrow?"

"It's not like you sleep, don't be ashamed now. You then already did what you was goin do or at least that's how you trying to play it."

"Why do we have to indulge on the past?"

"For all I know the past could've been yesterday even today."

"Her name was Halo."

"Now tell me how long."

"Does it matter?"

"Answer the question Maxwell Jonah!"

"You ain't gotta say my whole name loud enough for the whole world to know."

"Get to it? Maybe I should start acting crazy and deranged so you can take me seriously."

"You straight. I've been fooling around with her for almost two years."

"Did you have sex with her in my house?"

"I wouldn't do that to you Sunset!"

"That doesn't mean you didn't. I thought you wanted a clean slate with me, but you don't because if you did you would be singing like a canary right now instead of avoiding all of my questions. That's okay because I want my best friend back whether you like it or not." Max already knew what that meant. If Lana and Sunset hung out they was probably going to go clubbing, start drinking, smoking weed, and all the other peccadillo she had been secluded from. Then Max thought about the day that Sunset was giving birth then looked at her then looked away.

"A cat got your tongue or something because any other time you talk fine to me."

"It happened one time." Sunset rolled her eyes in the back of her head and they just sat back there so she started inhaling and exhaling.

"You disgust me," Sunset left Max in the bed contemplating her next move, her next question, even better silence and distance.

-

"Look who's here in the flesh," Infiniti grabbed Gunz so that he was embracing her body from the front and both of them were facing Chariot.

"Get out!" Gunz yelled, Chariot didn't budge, but a couple of tears did as she starting singing Did U Wrong by Pleasure P.

"I don't want to lose this relationship so we gotta stay strong, don't want to move on. I know you sick and tired of the fussing, the fighting, and the cussing, but I love you and you love me too. I did you wrong, you did me wrong." That was as far as Chariot got before Gunz laid hands on her.

"Do you know what dey do to liars in my country?" Gunz asked hemming Chariot's face up to the wall.

"No," she claimed in a very uncomfortable position wondering what was going to happen next. Feeling like Gunz was about to do something horrific to her.

"Dey cut dey tongues out for lying, but don't worry I got something else I'm going to do to you." Infiniti just sat there on the bed like she was his little sidekick watching Gunz at work and waiting for him to strike Chariot once again. Gunz grabbed Chariot's hand and turned it so that her palm was upright and started digging his sharp nails which probably felt like claws deep into Chariot's heart line until blood started gushing out and Chariot gave a bloody howl. Even though, she didn't know Infiniti she expected to fight her or something, but Infiniti was just cool and collective the whole time. In some sort of fashion Chariot kind of admired that because if it was her sitting on the bed she probably would've reacted differently.

All Chariot did was lie so you can just imagine what was going to happen to Infiniti with her deceitful ass. Infiniti couldn't believe Chariot actually thought she was going to sing her way out of trouble. She had a good voice in all, but Gunz was too hardcore to let Chariot get away with her deception. He had too many principles, beliefs, and a bloody way of life for that shit. As this was happening the threat that Gunz posed to Infiniti didn't even register in her head like she was untouchable, but she could bleed too and Gunz made that clear towards Infiniti before he let Chariot go. Infiniti wasn't fazed by his little bloody mess not one bit. Chariot still had a chance to defend herself even though it was a life or death situation messing with Gunz. Guess she felt her life was more important. Infiniti on the other hand would've probably gambled with her life.

"Now get out and don't come back!" Gunz roared at Chariot. She ran down the stairs upon her release and fled to her car so she could go to the hospital before she bled to death. Chariot was in awe; a man had never brought her such agony before. It was like she wasn't bleeding anymore even though she was. She thought Gunz would've at least forgiven her since all she did was lie, but a lie to a Jamaican was like death. And it was all in the matter of if Chariot was just going to let their 15 month old relationship just go like that. As far as Infiniti goes, the mood was ruined not to mention Gunz was wiping up Chariot's blood so Infiniti just got fully clothed.

"I think I'm going to go now."

"Why are you leaving so soon? Did I beat it up that good?" *Hardly, sike naw you did stroke the shit out of me though while it lasted.*

"I can't complain or nothing and I would stay for round 2, but I got a doctor's appointment early in the morning and I wouldn't want you to get me in trouble with the doc."

"Oh, no I feel you I won't keep you go ahead and go home." Just as Infiniti was exiting Gunz' house Chariot was just pulling off to go check herself into the hospital and get a line full of stitches. The nearest hospital was 10 minutes away, but Chariot made it there in 5. She ripped a piece of her shirt to wrap her hand up for the time being while she filled out her hospital papers. Thereafter, she was seen and prepped for her stitches in no time, but the pain didn't bother her especially not after getting a tattoo on her spine, but the doctor wouldn't stop asking her questions.

"Did somebody stab you?"

"It's not really none of your business so can you just do your job and get this over with."

"Actually if we see any signs of neglect or abuse we are supposed to report them to police."

"You can make a report if you want too, but I'm not. The police can't help me neither can you, but you can stitch up my hand."

"You must really love this man to protect him like this."

"I'm not protecting him." The doctor wrapped Chariot's palm up with some white medical wrapping paper.

"I see many girls like you every day with worst conditions then you." And that was the last thing Chariot heard before she was halfway out the door especially since she was contemplating on where she was about to lay her head.

"Wait let me write you a script for pain." Chariot hoped the doctor wouldn't give any more lectures while he wrote out the script, and he didn't. He just wrote the script, handed it to her, and she dipped. Most likely, she was going to need the Tylenol 3's tonight when the numbing medicine wore off. Chariot didn't have time to stop at a drugstore so she just let the script linger in her purse. She decided to drive to the job and find one of the strippers there to make friends with.

Being a stripper you would think Chariot would think Chariot would go stay at a hotel, with family, or something since she had that stripper money. Plus Gunz was taking care of her, but her money was untouchable, and family wasn't because her family blacklisted her for being a stripper. She put all of her money in an IRA account so it could keep building interest. She had to budget her touchable money wisely because she was on a stripping hiatus until her hand healed.

Heading for De Ja Vu, Chariot knew there was going to be somebody there when she arrived, she just didn't know who. And even though strippers were the last people Chariot should be trusting let alone coworkers, she didn't have any room to be selective. There was hardly any traffic out on Chariot's long drive so she sped up and split her drive in half.

When she arrived back to De Ja Vu you could tell it was still jumping by the parking lot. All the parking spaces were occupied, street parking was gone, cars were still pulling up, and the thugs and the g's were still hanging around the entrance. Stepping back into her place of business, Chariot skimmed through the room, then she went in the dressing room like she was about to get changed to go to work. She saw this one girl whose named started with a C who she spoke with from time to time. She appeared to be getting ready to go home so Chariot singled her out to the side.

"What's up girlie?" Right away the girl gazed down noticing Chariot's bandaged hand.

"What's up with your hand?" The girl asked.

"I grazed my hand earlier."

"Yea right band-aids are for grazes. It looks like you had an operation on that thing. You shouldn't be here. What you waiting around here for?"

"I need a spot to crash at. I ain't got nowhere to go."

"How are you evicted or homeless working here?"

"My boyfriend put me out and it's been a real crazy night. You got room for me at your place or nah?"

"I don't even know you like that baby girl, but I guess you can fall through. I live with my boyfriend, but he's out of town."

"Thanks girl."

"I hope you don't ask strangers for housing every day. You better go get you a voucher or something or hurry up and get back on that pole for a security deposit."

"This is just as awkward for me as it is for you. I had the perfect life yesterday."

"I'm sure so how'd you get here? You drove with your one good hand?"

"Yeah I did. Thank goodness I'm even-handed. By the why what's your name again? I know it starts with a C."

"It's Chenille."

"And I'm Chariot." Chariot exited the club toe to toe with Chenille. Their fellow strippers were too caught up in their pole tricks to gossip about Chariot and Chenille. Chariot concealed her hand behind her purse so it could go unseen. Eventually, she was going to have to explain to her boss why she was going to be M.I.A for about 2 weeks. Her boss was probably going to inform everybody so either way it went she was going to be a hot topic.

On the freeway Chariot kept up with Chenille just fine who drove like a Russian. She leaned back in her seat, she cut some people off, she switched lanes numerously, and she kept her same speed the whole time. It was no way she could spare getting lost so she stayed as close to her as possible. At the end of her voyage Chariot ended up somewhere in Bloomfield Hills in the Windermere Hills at a spacious house. Chariot didn't really like hotels since she performed at a couple of hotels and motels in her lifetime. Some of her experiences at those places were ratchet so she was grateful to be at somebody's house on the hill. Parking in the driveway, Chariot followed Chenille in, thanked her once again, and complemented her house. Chenille just showed Chariot where she was sleeping.

"Do you have anything I can borrow to sleep in?"

"Yeah, let me go get a t-shirt for you." Chenille threw a white tee on the bed and left Chariot alone. Chariot undressed to the t-shirt and tried to get cozy, but her stitched up hand was aching and the numbness was starting to fade. She didn't want to bother Chenille so she just channeled the pain like a trooper. She finally ended up falling asleep on her back with a pillow stuffed adjacently under her hand.

-

When Infiniti reached her house at about 1:26AM it was no way in hell she was going to go straight to sleep without showering. Infiniti wasn't one to stress herself out, but it was time for her to rethink the men in her life especially since their women were starting to sweat her more than her gym membership was. Especially the chick Tame so Infiniti bathed, put on a sports bar, a pair of yoga pants, pulled out her yoga mat, turned on a CD with the sounds of water, and started doing yoga exercises. She thought to herself in the yoga spirit for a whole hour straight. Afterwards she went straight to sleep. Guess a good mental workout like yoga can exhaust you.

Chapter 11: Late Nights, Early Mornings

After a couple of eyelid flutters, Max looked over his shoulder to see he was the only dweller in his bed. He hoped he hadn't upset Sunset to the point of no return. All he could think about was how he could fix his mistakes so he called Halo to fully elaborate on his goodbye resolution even though Halo had already made goodbye as official as certified mail.

Picking up his phone, Max dialed Halo's number one last time. Halo was too sleepy to consider who was calling her. All that mattered was that her phone was ringing and since she heard it, she answered it. Max could tell Halo was half asleep.

"Come on Halo, get up, we need to talk."

Sunset fell asleep at the bottom of the stairs and began stretching trying to recuperate from last night's tension. It was time for her to get up, get dressed, and spend some time with her son. Her son was officially the only man in the world that would never hurt her.

Immediately, all of Halo's drowsiness went away once she recognized who was on the other end.

"We don't need to talk about anything."

"Why you tripping, I'm the one with the bad news."

"What bad news you got? You got 10 days to live or something? I wouldn't consider that as bad news."

This was new territory to Max, Halo and her anger. The only thing he was guilty of was having a wife. As Max continued to talk to Halo, Sunset was on her way up the stairs. She didn't hear Max's voice yet.

"That was cold as hell, why are you so angry with me?"

"Because you're a sorry excuse for a man and if you thought that was cold, you don't know what cold is."

"Who changed you overnight? What dude took you back so you don't need me anymore?"

"I woke up, that's what changed me. Thank you for your lessons and showing me how lame dudes behave themselves."

"Lame? That bozo you were shacking up with was lame that's why you kept coming back to me. You sure loved this lame D though!" By this time Sunset heard Max's voice she knew this was the best time to eavesdrop.

"The sex was good, but that's about it so whatever you called to tell me I hope you plan to get it off your chest in the next 60 seconds because I'm done with you and this conversation."

"How are you done with me after all I've done for you?"

"That's 55 more seconds."

"I just called to tell you I need to be there for my wife and my son, no more fooling around."

114

"That is the smartest thing you've said since I've known you. It wasn't a pleasure knowing you, but I'm happy to accept that now goodbye," Halo hung up the phone jigging on the bed for joy. She didn't even comprehend the part about his seed though.

Sunset still had a grudge against Max, but she was kind of pleased to hear that he was making moves to get his life right. She wondered if he was trying to outsmart her by pretending to get rid of his side chick. All she knew was they had a son together and that she had to make up her mind quick. Whatever decisions she made now was going to affect her son.

-

Infiniti's alarm went off 5 times already and still she was hiding under the covers. Maybe it was her dislike of doctors and check-ups that was keeping her asleep. Whether she liked it or not, it was time for her to get ready for her doctor's appointment. Infiniti hit the shower and did all the dressing no, no's. She had on a thong and was dressed like she was going to a music video audition. Usually the receptionist Meshell was chill, but once she saw Infiniti approaching her station, she practically threw the sign-in clipboard at Infiniti.

Opening up Meshell's window, Infiniti sent the clipboard flying at her like a flying saucer. It wasn't like Meshell could do anything, but get hit since her back was turned.

"What the hell?" Meshell yelled feeling the impact of the chart.

"Now we goin try this again. When I walk out this office and walk back in, I want you to hand this chart to me like you got some sense." Meshell rolled her eyes, but she couldn't risk losing her job so she obeyed Infiniti and handed her the chart nicely with a fake smile. Infiniti just signed her name just as calmly and nonchalant as ever and seated herself in the waiting area. She dug into the latest Essence Magazine, as two patients in the lobby were griming the life out of her.

Once the assistant called Infiniti to the back, they did all the pre-reqs. They checked her blood pressure, her weight, and made her pee in a cup. Infiniti wanted to book, but her appointment was nowhere near finish. Everything was fine until her sexy male doctor came in and gave her a pap exam which was so irritating, but very necessary.

"Everything looks good, is there anything you want to ask me?" Dr. Vice asked ready to wrap up.

"Yeah I'm going to need you write me a script to get some birth control." Dr. Vice couldn't believe his ears.

"Wow, I can't believe I'm hearing this from you. It took you long enough. You're too beautiful not to be sexually active and I'm glad you're going to use something besides condoms if you use condoms, whatever you do spare me the details." That's exactly why Infiniti loved her doctor. He didn't ask nosey questions about her sex partners, her sex capades, or anything concerning her sex life.

"I've been doing a little research and I want the Mirena. The 10-year one because none of them other methods are going to work for me."

"You have to be on your cycle to get that IUD so just call me when you come on your cycle and we'll get your IUD inserted."

"Thanks doc."

-

The last thing Chariot was thinking about was waking up especially after she just lost her boyfriend and paid a price for it at the hospital. Her newfound friend Chenille was clearly not a good choice. Whether Chariot wanted to wake up or not, the boys in red and blue were about to knock her door down. The longer Chariot took to get up, the less time she would have to get away from the handcuffs, the interrogation rooms, and police cars they were about to be in the back of if Chariot didn't break a leg.

Chenille shook Chariot four times before she got up trying to ask questions and do the wake up thing. Chenille yanked Chariot by her good hand down into the basement and through an underground passageway that led to freedom. Chariot had no idea what was going on, but could only imagine. All she could do now was go with the flow. She hoped that her car wouldn't get seized, impounded, or a boot on it.

The po-po's would never find this way, not even with the blueprint of the house. Chenille's secret passageway was hidden like a panic room, an underground railroad, or a revolving bookcase type of thing. By the time the police discovered the hidden gateway Chariot and Chenille would be long gone and either way it went, the police were dealing with a lose-lose case. The authorities would never have enough evidence to lock her up under a cell nor was Chenille going to give them an opportunity to try their luck. The end of the passage led into Chenille's neighbor house Mica. Chariot couldn't believe what she was seeing. All this time she thought that Gunz had exposed her to a world of tribulation, but never did she have to run.

Chenille's fiancé Lorenz who was known on the street as LR was locked up a year ago for violating his probation. LR cut a deal with the dirty crackers to get an early release, but he had no intentions of keeping the end of his bargain. He just wanted to be free and freedom is what he got. The police wanted LR to help them do the impossible. They wanted LR to help them take down his top enemy Wayne, which was going to be tricky because LR was not a poser. He wasn't about to snitch on nobody, he wasn't about to work for no cracker, and he wasn't about to flaunt himself around his arch enemy. So LR got over on the cops, they chalked it up, but now that Wayne is dead, and they know LR was his top enemy, they trying to stick him with murder. Chenille and LR knew the cops were going to be coming, they just didn't know when.

-

Thumbs were down, because Lola didn't like her private amateur night rendezvous with Cardi. This barter deal was strictly between sex and a widescreen DVD. Lola couldn't cognize why Dakota was so coconuts over her basic bae. Where were relationship standards when you needed them? With women like Dakota in subsistence, females need to take standardized relationship courses.

Lola called Dakota so she could come through and dish out a bunch of tears.

"Hey Lola," Dakota answered sure it was that magic phone call she had been waiting all night for.

"Hey, how you holding up today?"

"I'm good, but what happened?" Dakota should've already known what happened because Cardi got home super late if he even went home. Guess she still wanted to believe he wasn't a cheater.

"I'm sorry Dakota, but we did it, and if you ask me I don't think this is the first time Cardi slept with somebody else." Hearing those words made Dakota want to ball up her fists and beat up Cardi in his sleep, but she didn't.

"What makes you say that?" Dakota asked wondering how Lola felt she knew Cardi better than her. Just because you sleep with somebody one time doesn't mean you know them. Just because you live with somebody or you've been with somebody for years doesn't mean you know them either.

"Cardi did not resist this opportunity. He was like when? Where? Come on, let's go. I played my part and he played his. Not to mention he told me he wanted to do this again. I told him it was a onetime thing, and he didn't show me any signs of regret." Dakota wondered if Lola was lying now, even though she was telling the whole truth, and nothing but the truth.

"Well I'm about to get up and be over there so I can pick it up. I'll just call you when I get in the car."

"Alright then see you." Lola was interested in what Dakota was going to do with the tape, and her relationship with Cardi. She wondered if Dakota was going to sit Cardi down and play the tape for him so she could memorize his facial expression when he realized that he was setup by his own girlfriend. Being a male he would probably try to flip the script on her. She wondered if Dakota was about to confront Cardi before she came to pick up the tape or if she was just going to let him be, but nines out of ten she figured Dakota would probably be naïve and stay with him. And she wondered if Dakota was going to hate her for subduing her man even though she dared her too.

Washing up, Dakota questioned who Cardi was because he was starting to have immoral qualities. Qualities that probably already existed; she was just too blinded by his goodness to notice them. Here Dakota was shooting moves to catch Cardi while he was laying in the bed sleep like he did a night-shift on somebody's payroll. Remembering everything Lola had told her, Dakota wondered how many others were there, and if he had sexed anybody else up that worked at the club. There was no way

120

in hell Dakota was going to be able to trust Cardi now sleep or awake. Getting in the car, Dakota called Lola back just as she said she would.

"Alright where you stay at?" Dakota asked soon as she picked up.

"I stay in Fountain Park in Westland on 37410 Fountain Park Circle."

"Got you in my GPS, I'll be calling you back in a minute." Dakota made it to Lola's house just fine and Lola came outside exactly when Dakota called so she wouldn't miss her. Once Dakota saw her standing around the front pasture she pulled into a parking space and went inside her house. She couldn't help, but feel queasy knowing that Cardi cheated on her in the same space she was walking in. She didn't know what she was going to do with the tape yet or when she was going to watch it really. All that she knew was that she had to get it in her possession. She wondered if Lola had watched the tape yet. Did she have multiple copies of it? Have she done something like this before since she cooperated so well? How did she just know Cardi was going to dive into her sheets headfirst? Hypothetically thinking wasn't going to get Dakota nowhere. Dakota followed Lola in and took a seat on her couch.

"I'm not going to stay for long. I just want the tape and I'm a go."

"I thought we were going to chat a little bit."

"I really don't have anything to talk to you about anymore." Lola couldn't believe Dakota was all snappy all

121

of a sudden, but she figured she was upset. Clearly Dakota didn't know who to be angry with so she let it go and just went and got the tape. Being in the apartment was too much for her so when Lola got back to the living room from getting the tape Dakota was standing by the door.

"Damn you ain't have to go stand by the door. If I would've known you were going to act like this I wouldn't have even invited you in. You really don't want to be here do you?"

"No I don't, but thank you for the tape though." Dakota snatched it out of Lola's hand which was unnecessary and there was nothing she could say to defend that.

"You should've left your attitude at my rug; good vibes only. You the one that dared me to sleep with your insignificant other. I just made a joke and you took it and turned it into something else. But if you want to be angry with me go ahead because that's still not going to fix your problem at home with your boyfriend." Dakota didn't say another word. She just turned around and purposely bopped Lola with her purse on her way out. Lola just closed the door behind her.

"That bitch bugging, her man better not call me either because I'm going to tell him a thing or two." Dakota didn't think about how her actions could affect her job or Cardi, but it was a lose-lose situation because even if she kissed Lola's ass she was going to do whatever she wanted to do regardless. Going home Dakota watched the tape and cried because Cardi was a first class cheater, but she made sure she ejected it out the DVD player and hid it somewhere.

Chapter 12: Reckless Thinking

Dakota and Cardi haven't been the same and probably want be the same ever again all because of Infiniti and the rest of them. Infiniti's destructive relationship forces didn't really even matter in this situation because their relationship was destroyed long before Infiniti. Dakota just couldn't see it yet, and even though Infiniti doesn't ultimately set out to destroy relationships; she always does and enjoys the thrill of a broken heart.

Cardi was tired of sleeping in the doghouse, and he was tired of having blue balls. He was bored with Dakota's cookie and even though he was doing his thing on the side, the more distant Dakota was, the greater Cardi's hormones shifted towards his other women. Since Lola was still on his brain Cardi tried his luck even though she made it clear that it was a one-time thing.

"What the hell are you calling me for?"

"Whoa, chill, shorty. That's how you talk too dudes you smash?"

"Cardi, I smashed you as a bet. The bet is over, I won and your girl lost."

"I don't understand riddles so stop riddling me like I'm a board game or something."

"Dakota and I played you. She challenged me to sleep with you so I did and she asked me to record it so I did. What did you think I was interested in you as a person?"

"You dirty for that. Y'all dirty for that. I don't know why I expected anything less from two thong rich jazzabelles."

"Thanks a million, so is your mother." After that remark Cardi briskly ended his call with Lola. He wasn't convinced Dakota was conspiring against their relationship; otherwise he wouldn't have a house life or a relationship. Just like a man, he shrugged it off and called his next resort which was Infiniti positive she wouldn't downgrade him or turn him down. Sneaking outside on the porch Cardi called Infiniti and she answered right away.

"What's shaking Cardi, hardy?"

"Nothing much Infiniti, amenity."

"Finally flipped the bird on your girl and your barracuda?"

"Yep especially since you've been running through my mind all day."

"I then told you about using your corny pickup lines on me. I can tell English wasn't your strong suite."

"I meant to tell you your legs were looking so scrumptious the other day like you just rubbed baby oil and Vaseline all over them."

"Never give a woman a late complement."

"So what time do they open?"

"Ha, ha, ha always cracking jokes. Come see me and they'll open right up soon as you say open sesame."

'Dakota peeked out the window and watched Cardi talk on the phone roaming in the parking lot. She was curious who he was flirting with and if it was somebody new or somebody old because you never know with him. The only names she knew were Lola and Infiniti, but there could be so many more names she didn't know.

"Girl you know the right things to say and how to say them."

"What's stopping you from coming to see me right now?"

"Nothing that's why I'm about to get ready, I'm a scoop you up, and then we can go grab a bite because my stomach growling and we can map it out from there. What you got a taste for?"

"Ummm... I got a taste for some Red Lobster."

"Yeah that does sound good."

"Okay I'll see you in a minute." Once Infiniti got off the phone she got dressed, dressed for one man. Little did she know that one man wasn't going to cut it because it was more than one man who would see her, and it was going to be a couple of females too. Infiniti threw on a crop top and capris, the matching accessories, and stilettos. She threw some spiral curls in her hair, sprayed her body with some Ralph Lauren Romance, grabbed a Gucci baggete, and topped off everything with some diamonds personalized by her jeweler. Infiniti knew she was going to give Cardi a run for his money.

Meanwhile Dakota just sat on the bed and watched as Cardi got ready for his mysterious date. Dakota tried to bite her tongue, but she couldn't keep the top over her boiling anger. Her anger spilled over and she opened her mouth.

"Can we be real Cardi, where are you going?" Cardi didn't know why Dakota was suddenly so suspicious, but he knew he had to cover his tracks so he did the only thing he thought he could do to make himself look innocent which was a lie.

"I'm going out with the boys. I'm sorry I don't have an address ready for you, and a permission slip to sign." Dakota knew Cardi was getting ruthless because he never spoke to her in a tone so high with words so steep. And she knew Cardi wouldn't be dressed as sharp as he was dressed or going through the measures he was going through to hang out with the homies. She knew only a woman could make a man get dressed like that.

"You don't have to be so rude you know. I was just asking a question."

"I said I'm going out with the fellas. I don't say anything when you go out with your girls so what's the problem?"

"I don't go out with my girls first of all. Where are you and your boys going to go in the middle of the afternoon besides to see some old hoes?"

"Oh so you think I'm cheating?" Dakota wasn't trying to spill anything so she just corrected herself and stopped nagging. She took a deep breath.

"I'm sorry baby just have fun okay."

"Okay I'll see you later baby." Cardi yelled from the door not trying to give Dakota no kiss or no hug since he was growing use to not being affectionate with her anyway.

"Bye!" Dakota yelled back like everything was okay. When she heard Cardi lock the apartment door she counted a couple of Mississippi's in her head, got her steel baseball bat out the front closet, unlocked and relocked the door, and took cover to her car. Cardi was busy fooling around with his sounds so Dakota went undetected. If only he would've saw her jetting to her car. Finally, when Cardi took off, Dakota did too sure she was going to catch somebody.

-

Harlan decided to treat himself to lunch at his nearest Red Lobster located on Novi Road. He just scored some major companies on an account he would have to do major graphic design and website building for. He was single and hated the single life. He figured maybe he could meet a pretty waitress or somebody dining since he couldn't cook worth a lick. Harlan never had to cook because that was Halo's specialty, but Halo wasn't there anymore, and as bad as he hated to say it he kind of missed the girl. There was no way he was going to settle for a woman whore, and as far as Infiniti goes he was too disappointed in her to even think about her even though Infiniti made it clear how she felt about relationships from the get-go.

Harlan ended up being seated with a nice non-smoking table by the window. It practically killed the man to be a loner, but better to be a loner then a sucker for both of the women in his life.

-

"Bitch we barely made it in the house," Chenille complained to her girl Mica.

"Who is this you got with you?" Mica wondered noticing Chariot because she was turned on by her sexiness.

"Oh this is somebody I dance with named Chariot. She needed somewhere to crash last night." Already two pieces of details were gone in one sentence. Chariot hoped Chenille didn't tell her neighbor anything else about her.

"Bet you wish you would've found somewhere else to crash now huh?"

"I guess," Chariot answered not knowing where to turn or what to do next.

"I'm not trying to involve you in me and my fiancé's mess or nothing, I was just trying to be a friend. I really didn't know when they were coming. I know you should be resting, but at least you've got your exercise for the day." Chariot did wish she had slept somewhere else last night, but she tried to laugh it off."

"Ha-ha, you got jokes."

"What happened to your hand?" Mica's snooping ass wondered.

"No offense, but I don't care to share." Mica really wanted to know so she could go kick whoever ass did that to her. Whoever messed up her future wife's hand.

"I know you not ashamed everybody goes through some kind of abuse in their life. I'm just asking out of concern because I think it happened last night." Chenille had dipped off to another room to call Lorenz and tell him about the latest events without warning so it was just Chariot and Mica.

"Since you know Chenille you can crash here anytime you need too. All I ask is that you treat me and my house with respect." Chariot felt real uneasy about staying there with Mica, but she was too cheap to nitpick.

"Okay I would appreciate that." Chenille failed to tell Chariot that Mica was a lesbo and Mica probably liked Chariot that's why she invited her to stay. Matter fact Mica definitely liked Chariot, but she was too caught up in her own drama to notice.

"Okay I just got off the phone with my future husband LR and he's good. I'm good, everybody's good now, so why don't we go get some lunch because I'm starving," Chenille claimed rubbing her stomach.

Chenille and Mica were dressed, but Chariot wasn't. She still had on the t-shirt Chenille gave her the night before.

"Hello, I'm not dressed," Chariot looked around.

"What you wear a size 3?" Mica figured filling her eyes up with Chariot's body.

"Yeah how'd you know?" Mica just gave Chariot a smirk.

"Just follow me and pick whatever you like. I got everything you'll need," and when Mica said that she meant it. Chariot threw a nice little piece together out of Mica's spare closet and put her sexy face on like she wasn't wounded even though she was. Chenille knew the police were still hot around there, so she distinguished herself a little so she wouldn't endanger anybody. Off to Red Lobster they went on Novi Road.

-

It was hard for Tame to hear with all the noise Halo was making downstairs. She couldn't name what Halo was doing right off the back so she got out of the bed surprised she didn't hear Tatum getting up, and went to Halo's room so she could find out firsthand.

130

"What the hell is going on?" Tame scared Halo from just popping up in her room without knocking on the door.

"I'm sorry if I woke you sis, I'm just overjoyed right now."

"You and Harlan getting back together or something because I'll give you a couple more days here, but don't forget your time is quickly running out." The living agreement they made had completely slipped Halo's mind and it changed Halo's whole aura.

"Harlan and I aren't getting back together ever, and that leaves me assed out. I know we had a deal, but I don't have any other place to go, and now the bastard I was messing with has crossed himself out of my life which I am too thankful for."

"Oh that must've been the one putting his paws on you?"

"Does it really matter Tame?" There goes that stubbornness. Halo hated to admit when she was wrong and was still withholding information. It wasn't like Tame knew Max or Infiniti she thought.

"It does matter. Why can't we ever have a decent conversation without you getting all offended? When people are mad they vent so let's go out to my favorite restaurant so we can start venting."

"I guess."

Neither Halo nor Tame hung out in the mirror long before they were ready to hit the streets unlike some people who take hours and days just to go somewhere. They must've been reading each other's mind because they ended up putting the same color on.

-

While Infiniti was on her way to grab a bite, her little mentor thing was going out the window because Tier was about to go to jail for grand theft auto. God forbid anything else happen to her little country bumpkin.

Chapter 13: Closer to My Enemies

Infiniti was slipping and falling. Usually you couldn't pay her not to be aware of her surroundings. She was always looking in her rearview mirror, and would even use the sun visor mirror to spot out followers. She wasn't too concerned about Cardi and his girl even though she just might be the worst apple out the whole bunch. When Cardi reached Infiniti's extravagant house, Dakota took her little time to scribble down Infiniti's house address and store it in her memory. Even Cardi wasn't paying any attention either because it was his girlfriend, he knew what kind of car she drove, she was either right behind them or one car away, and he still didn't see her. He might have had a bad bitch in the passenger seat, but cheaters should always be on the lookout.

Red Lobster was crowded as usual because it was a five star restaurant and it attracted eaters from all the nearby cities. Dakota just watched Cardi as he opened up the car door and the restaurant door for Infiniti politely. Once they were inside she struggled on how she was going to make her entrance. In a way she wanted to grab a table that was close to theirs, but that was too traditional so she decided she would give them about 30 minutes to sip and eat, and bust in on them, drag her man out the restaurant by his ears, and leave Infiniti by herself to hitch a ride if everything went accordingly, but nothing ever went as planned.

Infiniti and Cardi sat in a section right by Harlan. Right when Infiniti and Cardi were seated Chariot and her crew arrived. They were seated in the back of the restaurant and after them came Tame and Halo who was seated in the middle of the restaurant, but that was just the beginning. Each of these tables had the same waitress. Infiniti could tell she was a gutter baby off rip by the way she introduced herself.

"Like my nametag say, my name is Christie. What y'all goin order and what y'all want to drank?" The waitress asked as she sat the menus down and pulled out her little pen and pad. Infiniti didn't tolerate illiterate or ghetto females on no occasion, but long as Christie didn't jack up their order or have a snotty attitude she was good.

"You don't have to give me a menu I already know what I want," Infiniti claimed.

"Go ahead," the waitress grabbed the menu back while Cardi tried to pick something.

"You can start me off with a lemonade and I would like the chicken alfredo."

"Do you know what you want now mister?" Cardi ordered a lemonade too and some shrimp and crab legs.

"Okay I'll bring y'all drinks and biscuits and y'all food should be up shortly." Cardi grabbed Infiniti's hand and started sweet talking her after Christie left and went to one of her other tables. Infiniti was a taker not a caker so she found her way out of that for the moment, and made her way to the ladies room where she had to walk right past Harlan who had his eyes fixed on all the other tables, and the aisle ways. There was no way Harlan was going to miss Infiniti walking by indeed he saw her leaving her table.
"I wonder what his story is." Harlan greeted green with envy of Infiniti's new companion still mad at her for not wanting to be with him. Infiniti stopped in her tracks right in front of Harlan's table. She didn't expect to see him

here at all, but she looked around for a minute to make sure he was talking to her.

"What the hell is that supposed to mean?"

"What he doing that I ain't doing? Oh yeah you just being the other woman right. I'm a good looking man and I got money so what else do you need?"

"Are you that shallow and pathetic you got to sit back and compare yourself to somebody else. Don't you worry about what that jawn doing or what I'm doing with him. Ain't nothing different I treat him just like I treated you. I don't want a relationship with you or him or anybody so stop whining and get over it! Envy doesn't look that good on you." Harlan just cut his eyes at Infiniti.

"Oh that's how it is now huh? You just screw um, suck um, and leave? I thought you were better than Halo, but you just as dirty as she was," Harlan turned up his face.

"Does it look like my feelings are hurt? I mean really just look at my face. You think I give a rat's ass about an insult?" Cardi looked towards the ladies room to see if he saw Infiniti coming out. Instead he saw Infiniti talking to some man at a table, but he didn't have any rights to go over there and interrupt their conversation like Infiniti was his girl because she wasn't. Besides he knew Infiniti was a beautiful woman, what man in his right mind wouldn't want a piece of her action?

"Look Harlan we're done talking." Infiniti kept going to her intended location. *He got me f'd up trying to analyze my actions and get all mouthy with me. If he wants a relationship he better go makeup with his bitch. I ain't got time for that shit. He was talking big shit too like he*

135

was going to do something to me. I wish somebody would. I gotta watch out for that jawn because he is too hooked. This probably ain't goin be the last time I see him either.

It was twenty minutes left before Dakota surfaced.

Once Christie reached Chariot's and the rest of them table it was a breeze. Nobody knew that Infiniti was in the same joint as them eating all classy and shit with another girl's man like always. And even though it was a small world, she was going to get away with it.

"Sis I never thought you would have marital problems."

"Me neither."

"So who did it?"

"That bitch Infiniti!" Tame made sure she put emphasis on the word bitch too. At the time Halo was about to take a swallow of some sprite, but when she heard Tame's last words she spit it right out. Some went on the table, some went on Tame, and some went on Halo.

"Was you choking or something?" Tame got up to pat Halo on her back.

"I wasn't choking I just couldn't swallow right after you mentioned that trick, chick Infiniti."

"Please don't tell me you know her too."

"Know her? She was sleeping with Harlan. She had sex with him right in front of my face like I was a spider on the wall." Halo got real irate.

"I swear if I ever see that low class hoe again I'm going to shove her face into a mirror!"

"Does the Infiniti you describing have gray eyes, cherry black hair, a medium brown skin complexion kind of like a pecan, like 5'6', and think she the shit?" Tame said even louder.

"Sounds just like that bitch!" People were starting to complain. Being the ghetto girl Christie was she just let them be, but as more and more complaints start piling up, the manager went in for the kill.

"I'm sorry, but I'm going to need you guys to leave."

"We ain't doing nothing, but talking like everybody else," Halo answered.

"Yes, but everybody can hear y'all conversation, and the vulgar language we don't permit in our restaurant."

"We didn't even get our food yet."

"Y'all didn't pay for it either and now that y'all about to leave drinks on us, just go," the manager looked around embarrassed.

"That's okay y'all got some nasty ass food anyway, and me and my sis got things to discuss!" Halo grabbed her purse along with Tame and they left 10 minutes before Dakota was going to surface.

"So Chariot what happened to your hand?" Chenille and Mica surprised her with the question out of the blue.

Chariot didn't want them two chatter bugs to be all up in her business so she made up a white lie.

"I was cutting some stuff up for a salad and cut myself" Mica and Chenille looked at each other instantly cracking up.

"I guess you think we were born in 1999. If you really don't want to tell us just don't. I can't say that means were going to stop asking you because I'm not, but you have no reason to lie or be ashamed." Infiniti bypassed Chariot's table strutting her stuff like Chariot was immobile. Out the corner of her cloudy eyes she knew exactly who she was upon. Faces was just something she didn't forget, and she knew when she was being followed which was funny because she was still clueless about the girl who had been following her every since she left her house. *Damn is this the only restaurant open today or just a small world? I guess that bitch can't be too hurt since she about to eat good. All I know is that bitch better not step up.*

Chariot was sitting right by the wall so she excused herself from the table and followed right behind Infiniti to the bat cage, not knowing Infiniti was one step ahead of her. Infiniti let Chariot walk into the bathroom, but once she was in she slammed the bathroom door closed and locked it making Chariot spin around.

"Why the hell are you following me? Didn't you bleed enough last night for me and you both?"

"I know your scheme, schemer. You think you got immunity because he digging you right now?"

"I am the least bit worried about Gunz because if he tries some Jamaican shit on me like that it's going to be chitty, chitty bang, bang for his ass."

"Well I just wanted a one-on-one with you. I think we both can help each other out."

"Sorry, but I work alone."

"Just think about it, one day you goin need some back up." Even though Infiniti got Chariot busted, Chariot admired her for everything she stood for. She was like a Harley Quinn.

Dakota had just hit her car alarm and was walking through the restaurant doors with a baseball bat trying to scope out Cardi who was wondering if Infiniti had fell in the toilet and needed somebody to help her out or maybe she wanted Cardi to come into the bathroom so they could get their freak on so he left his table and headed for the ladies room. Lucky for Chariot and Infiniti nobody had knocked on the door yet, but out of nowhere Infiniti's cell phone start ringing.

"Hold on please," Infiniti paused Chariot with her finger as she leaned against the door.

"Hello."

"Hey Infiniti guess what I did?" Tier bragged all geeked up.

"This is not a good time Tier."

"You'll be proud of me though. If you could just listen to me for a minute I can tell you."

"What did you do?"

"I stole his car," Tier continued just knowing Infiniti was going to congratulate her and she would win some cool points.

"Stole whose car?"

"My ex, the one I was telling you about Christion."

"What? We don't steal cars; we get money and buy them out of pocket. Why on Earth would you do some dumb shit like that!" Tier didn't expect Infiniti to yell at so crucially.

"Are you okay?" Cardi whispered tapping on the ladies room door looking over his shoulder to make sure he was crystal clear.

"Infiniti," Chariot tried to get her attention so Infiniti looked over at Chariot.

"Somebody's at the door for you."

"Tell him I'll be out in a minute," Chariot repeated the message just as Infiniti said it and Cardi went back to the table.

Dakota almost forgot how a restaurant was ran, but she got out of her trance quickly.

"Excuse me miss," the hostess tried to signal Dakota.

"I already have a table," Dakota said walking in quickly as possible to find Cardi and Infiniti and to keep her baseball bat undiscovered.

"Cardi Campbell where you at!" Cardi heard Dakota's voice nearby calling for him and she was yelling. He knew he was about to be in the doghouse forever. His next thought was to get the hell out of the restaurant. He could've warned Infiniti being almost right beside her that is, not that she couldn't handle her own, but at this point it was every man for himself. He got real low, stop drop and roll low and start heading for the exit about to dip without Infiniti. He made it all the way to his car without being spotted and zoomed off.

"Look Tier I got to go. Come on Chariot let's talk." Infiniti unlocked the ladies room door just on time because ladies were starting to head for the door. Infiniti led Chariot to the table she was sitting at. She was relieved Harlan wasn't at his table, but that didn't necessarily mean he was gone even though he was gone. She was glad she didn't have to worry about him prolonging her process though. When they arrived at the table the food was there, Cardi's drink was half full, but there no Cardi, and a berserk nut job with a bat ready to play softball with Infiniti's skull.

Chapter 14: Statistics and Catfights

Tame and Halo was still in the restaurant's parking lot like two lost little puppies. Tame couldn't remember where she parked, then Halo's shoe strings kept falling to her ankles and she kept bending over to tie them back up while Tame waited. Just as Tame pressed her car alarm she noticed Dakota's car and stopped Halo in her tracks.

"We need to talk to her so we goin wait here until she comes out."

"I'm not in the mood to wait for nobody Tame."

"This is another Infiniti statistic so chill out."

"Alright damn, should've got Micky D's, coney island, or something for all this bull crap."

Back in the restaurant Dakota start swinging her bat and each time she swung it she missed Infiniti. All Dakota did hit was a couple of martini and water glasses.

"I guess you didn't think I was going to find out!" Chariot helped Infiniti duck down and they crept the restaurant's floors just as low as Cardi had before he went estranged. *Damn, why am I so popular today!*

-

Speaking of Cardi, he made it to his townhouse safely without getting pulled over or threatened by his psycho girlfriend who was on a rampage. He also made it without Infiniti who was going to get his ass for leaving her stranded, without a ride, and with his madwoman. He had no idea that Dakota knew about his night with Lola. He wasn't man enough to face Dakota so he packed his bags, took Carmella up on her offer, hit the road, and turned off his cell phone. Guess there was no working out his relationship, no letter saying goodbye, and he said to hell with Infiniti. It's a first time for everything because no man ever said to hell with Infiniti before or pulled the sucker ass shit Cardi just pulled. He had a lot of money saved up from his DJ gig and he decided he would hibernate to Chicago with Carmella. In Chicago he was going to spend a couple of days at a hotelly and between those days and driving, there would be enough time to decide his next move.

-

    The managers and employees were hot on Dakota's tail, but they didn't want to get hit with the bat so they kept their distance.

    "Come on now Infiniti you a bad bitch face me like a real woman!" Infiniti wasn't fazed by Dakota or her bat since it was obvious the bat carrier knew her name so she rose to her feet.

    "Okay bitch if you're a woman you'll ditch the bat. And for the record wasn't nobody running from you because I don't even know who the hell you are!" Everybody was tuning into Dakota and Infiniti like they were a TV program.

    "Don't worry about who I am you know my man and that's all I need to know!" Infiniti looked at Dakota's face real hard realizing she was the girl who Cardi was talking to one night at the club.

    "Oh you're looking for Cardi so join the club because I'm looking for him too."

    "Don't play games with me like you don't know where he's at. I followed y'all ass the whole way here. And I know you know something. I remember you."

"So where is he then? Is he hiding in my purse? Do you wanna check the restrooms? Why don't you check the parking lot? You need to take your bat and your problems up with your little man child." Dakota thought real hard about that for a minute and realized that Infiniti was right yet again. Infiniti just walked past Dakota to where Chariot was sitting now as Dakota put her bat down and exited the restaurant before somebody called the police on her.

"I thought she was about to beat your ass," Chariot laughed.

"Please I can talk my way of anything. Mind if I take a seat?"

"Nope go ahead." While Infiniti was sitting down chatting she texted Gunz the address so he could scoop her up not because Chariot was in her face, but because that was an option.

On the way to the car Dakota saw Tame and Halo standing by her car.

"Why are y'all guarding my car? I got a car alarm for that!" Dakota was pissed from what just occurred, but Tame didn't expect Dakota to act like she didn't know who she was.

"What's wrong with you Dakota, I wanted to talk to you about Infiniti?"

"Look Tammy, I mean Tame, whatever just stay away from me. Forget Infiniti and all this mess I'm done with it." Dakota pulled off leaving her fumes all up in Tame's and Halo's nostrils. Wasn't nothing Tame and Halo could do either, but go home after they hit up a drive thru joint. Tame and Halo decided they were going to eat some Popeye's Chicken. Once they went home they were too exhausted to talk especially Tame after the way Dakota just dismissed her.

Back in the restaurant Chenille, Mica, Chariot, and Infiniti were just chit-chatting. Chariot didn't even notice how hard Mica was crushing on her since they left the house. She felt like it was love at first sight. She wanted to lick and suck on every part of Chariot's body if that was all Chariot would let her do, but if Chariot was willing she'll make her woman.

"Okay Chariot give me your number and I'm a call you." Chariot gave Infiniti her number, Gunz replied to Infiniti's text message saying he was outside so Infiniti copied the number and dipped.

-

Meanwhile, Tier got a hunch she was being followed so she turned down a side street and shot a left so the car behind her made a left. Then Tier made a right so the car behind her made a right too. Then Tier made a u-turn so they made a u-turn too, so Tier pulled over and the strange car did the same. Tier got out the car and walked up to the car behind her where she found herself getting knocked out by the girl's car door.

"You are one dumb hoe! I'm pulling up in my driveway and I see you pulling out in my man shit!" The strange girl with candy blonde hair stepped out the car and purposely stepped on some of Tier's fingers as she checked to see if her nose was broke with the other hand, but really it just had a few droplets of blood on it.

"Are you the retarded bitch that's been calling Christion lately because it's me bitch Riana the wifey! I guess you thought you were just goin joy ride in his car for the rest of your life huh?" Riana bent down to Tier's level where Tier head butted her making her fall back into her car. This is where Infiniti had Tier beat though, fighting wise. Tier could probably whoop a bitch's ass, but that was all she was use to was beating up bitches. A true bitch would do whatever she had to survive even if she was outnumbered male or female. Not to mention Tier was still in her feelings over Christion when he should've been collecting dust and cobwebs in the past. Even if she did want to get his attention, stealing his car sure as hell was a dumb ass way to do it.

-

Singing a radio tune Christion shot down the stairs to get his car keys out the key bowl, and lock-up, but in the back of his mind he was wondering why Riana hadn't come back yet. She was just supposed to be dropping off the latest books she edited to her girlfriend's company "Freaky Girl Books." Little did he know the drop-off had already been complete and she was doing some personal investigating? Christion knew how women could be just talk, talk, and talk so he didn't bother her. But it was when he locked the door behind him and noticed an empty driveway when he realized something was terribly wrong.

"Somebody then got me for my wheels!" I hope they don't think they goin get away with this." Immediately Christion unlocked the door back and searched through the house phone database so he could find his boy's number and when he found it he pressed talk. Automatically Christion assumed some thief borrowed his car because it was no way anybody in they right mind would steal from him because he was a goon.

"Aye Jodi we need to roll out ASAP so come scoop me." Jodi didn't ask any questions he just called some of the fellas out of the game room hopped in his truck and skirted off to Christion's street. Second phone call was to on-star who could track down his car much faster than he could. Christion jotted down the current location of his whip and shot outside where Jodi and the gang was awaiting which included Jodi the driver, Domino who was Jodi's youngest brother, Jazz who was Jodi's neighbor, and Christion.

"Where we headed to?" Jodi asked.

"Some asshole jacked my car here go the address right here," Christion handed Jodi the paper while Jodi hit his GPS and put the car in reverse. He stepped on the gas, pushed play on his remote control, while Jodi's bass set off every car alarm they drove by.

"I hope you know my man is probably right around the corner," Riana claimed.

"Good I've been waiting to see his ass." Tier circled Riana who was still shaking off the last hook she just took.

Out of nowhere Riana burst out laughing crookedly so Tier swung on her with a right hook.

"What the hell is so funny?"

"You know you then f'd up right?" Tier hit her with a left hook and Riana just took it. Hitting the corner Christion spotted his car, and saw Tier banging up Riana.

"You goin let your side chick beat up wifey like that?" Jodi asked cracking up because it was obvious he got carjacked by a girl and Riana went to the rescue.

"This shit ain't funny don't nobody cross a goon or lay a hand on my woman, but me come on y'all." Each one of the fellas opened up their door and broke up the little catfight that was going on.

147

"Domino and Jazz why don't y'all drive my car home," Christion tossed him the keys.

"Took you long enough baby," Tier said as Jodi held her by her arms trying to sound big and bad even though she was surrounded by a gang.

"Let me go Jodi this ain't got shit to do with you!" Let this had of been Infiniti, Jodi wouldn't have holding her no more.

"You alright baby. When you get in the car keep your eyes closed okay baby." Christion forewarned Riana picking her up and carrying her to the passenger side of her car and putting her inside.

"I'm good," Riana said trying to sound strong for her boo. After closing the door he got back to the point.

"Why couldn't you break up with me like a man Tier asked?"

"Shut the fuck up I don't want to hear that shit!" Jodi held on to Tier like she was a punching bag and Christion banged on her like he saw Tier banging on Riana.

"Nobody ever said we were in a relationship. We were just fucking and now we're not," Christion said boldly and coldly.

"This is exactly why I don't want you in my life now you don't know how to act," Christion figured knowing Tier couldn't talk at all through the thrashing he was giving her. She couldn't even mutter.

"And after today I don't want to ever see you again or next time you want live to see tomorrow."

Christion dumped Tier's body on the sidewalk. Her lip was busted, her eyes were swollen shut, her face was bloody, her nose was broken, and she probably had some fractured ribs. It didn't even bother Jodi to see a woman get beat so crucially. He felt kind of sorry for Tier because she looked like the black version of Pocahontas, and she was just retaliating because she had just gotten played. Guess goons are real heartless. Christion jumped in the whip with Riana and drove her home, and Jodi followed the way. When Christion arrived at his driveway he saw Domino standing by his car, but Christion was worried about wifey so he wasn't going to hit the streets today. He gave the go signal to his fellas, carried Riana in the house, even though she could walk. He didn't want her to walk, and he catered to her all day putting ice on her and cleaning her wounds.

-

When Dakota reached home she expected maybe Cardi would be there trying to beat her home, but she was fed up with him. She didn't care if he was or wasn't there, but on his behalf it would be better if he wasn't there. Eventually Dakota was going to miss him because that was her significant other and she was use to seeing his face, but she knew she was going to have to get over it. Going in the house she saw that some of Cardi's belongings were gone. She didn't know if Cardi left her was trying to stay away for a couple of days or what. There was no note anywhere. She quickly dialed his phone, pressing redial time after time, but all she got was the voicemail so she figured he powered his phone off. Dakota threw the house phone against the wall making the back part of the phone and the battery fall out.

"How the hell is he going to leave me when he cheated and how the hell is he going to act like I'm not supposed to be mad? I can't believe this shit!" Dakota started swinging and slanging the rest of Cardi's stuff around, but she remembered her aunt was vacationing in Chicago from a voicemail she had heard on her phone earlier that day. Feeling like she needed a vacation too she put the phone back together, and called Carmella to see if she could join her.

"Hi Aunt Carmella," Dakota fronted like she wasn't just throwing a bitch fit.

"Hi niecey pooh."

"How's it going down there in Chicago?"

"Everything's good and sunny."

"I was thinking maybe I could join you." Carmella couldn't believe her ears, and her first mind was to say no because it was obvious Dakota would ruin her plans with Cardi, but Carmella figured Dakota's arrival would be good. Carmella didn't even know about the absurdity that had just happened in their hometown about Lola or Red Lobster. She didn't know the main reason Cardi was fleeing Dakota was because he was in a whole heap of shit. All Carmella wanted her secret to be out in the open so she could have Cardi all to herself.

"Yes you sure can come on. You know that hotel we use to always stay at when we'll have our family trips in Chicago right?"

"I remember."

"Just come there and ask the hotel clerk for a key and come on up."

"Okay I'll call you when I get there."

"That will be great." Dakota didn't understand Carmella's excitement because she expected her to say no. Dakota packed a bunch of outfits, shoes, bikinis, perfumes, accessories, and other miscellaneous items and hit the road. If only she knew what she about to be getting into. And if only she knew Cardi had just arrived at the same hotel she was going too, and was on his way up the elevator to cuddle up with her auntie.

-

After Gunz picked Infiniti up from the restaurant their ride was real short and sweet, but Infiniti didn't care because she only wanted a ride anyway.

"I got to make a run so I'm going to have to drop you off at home queen."

"Awww I wanted to spend some time with you," Infiniti pretended to be hurt even though she wasn't and would rather be at home anyway.

"We can hook up later," Gunz said like Infiniti's poutiness didn't even affect him. Infiniti couldn't believe her fake sadness wasn't working. She told Gunz her address so she could get out of his hairs. On the way to her house she noticed a familiar body lying along the sidewalk just as Christion left her. Being the person she was you'll think she'll just drive on by especially since she didn't know Tier like that. She knew retribution would be great if she got involved since it was obvious Tier couldn't defend herself so she opted to be her hero.

"Hold on Gunz swing by the sidewalk I know that girl!" Gunz didn't really want to stop, but since he had his queen in the car with him, he pulled on over. Getting out Infiniti ran to Tier's side like that was her ace boon coon even though she didn't care about anybody, but herself.

Remembering Tier's phone call from earlier she realized it probably had something to do with that car ordeal.

"Tier who did this to you?" Tier wasn't responsive especially not seeing all the birds she just saw flying around in her head.

"Gunz help me put her in the car." After Gunz picked Tier up and put her in the car, he arrived at Infiniti's house in no time.

"I have a guesthouse on my property; I call it my safe house for situations like these. If you can please help me carry her back there. I know you gotta go so we won't go the long way."

"For sure queen." Gunz was the first male to ever step foot in her house only because he had to carry Tier.

"Thank you so much baby," Infiniti gave Gunz a hug and he smacked her on the booty before he left. After Infiniti secured the front door she cleared all the blood off of Tier's face and gave her a fresh cold rag every 30 minutes to compress on her eyes. She figured she'll bother her with some questions whenever she was ready to talk.

Chapter 15: 4 Wheel Drive

Today was an untainted day for Max and Sunset despite their marital differences. Sunset was in the clear past the postpartum stages so he could revive her sex drive. Sex was the furthest thing from her mind since her and Max was still on bad terms. Right before they went to the hospital Max took his daily dosage of ex. Even though he had to drive, even though there was no more Halo to give him a quick sexual eruption, even though he had to care for his son. Finally they were able to bring their son home, but that really wasn't going to do any justice for their upside down relationship. It was hard not to interact with someone who was constantly in your face, who you needed to communicate with for the sake of your child. Sunset didn't pay any attention to Max at all from the time they left the house to the time they got back to the house which eventually he got to the point where smoke was shooting out his ears.

"Sunset I know you hear me talking to you," Max said as they were settling the baby in his crib. Max was informing Sunset on how he was about to start a real job so she was going to be home alone more frequently which was nothing, but a cover up for gambling.

"I don't care Max," Sunset broke her silence.

"What you mean you don't care?"

"Don't start reporting when you come and go now. It's a little too late for that don't you think?"

"I'm trying to make things right with you," Max raised his voice.

"Okay so do yourself a favor and leave me alone. Long as your son is taken care of that's all you need to worry about right now because I'm still hurt by you. And I'm not going to slide it up under the rug today, tomorrow, or the day after that, but when I do you'll know." There was nothing Max could say about that so he just walked away.

-

Tier didn't have a clue where she was when she finally woke up. You'll think with the whooping she took she would've been hospitalized. Infiniti didn't do hospitals or doctors so Infiniti's best remedy for Tier was natural healing.

"Tier its okay, I found you on the sidewalk, but you're here with me now. What happened yesterday when you got off the phone with me?" Tier recognized Infiniti's voice. She couldn't believe Infiniti had found her and was housing her after she yelled at her over the phone.

"Why'd you pick me up? I thought you were mad at me."

"Yeah I was because I knew you were riding out and something like this could happen to you so can we get to that?"

"Well I stole Christion's car the dude that I was telling you about yesterday, and his girl Riana was following me the whole time so finally I stopped the car and then we started knucking and bucking and then Christion came and got his friend to hold me down while he did this to me."

"So did you beat the other girl ass?"

"Yeah I did."

"Well don't worry about it. You just get well and I'm a take care of it for you. Was there anybody else that was there that needs to be dealt with?" Tier thought back to yesterday.

"Yeah somebody named Jodi and somebody named Domino."

"I'm a get you a little CNA to take care of you because I ain't no babysitter. I can't sit by your bedside every day, but you can stay here until you get better."

"What did I do to deserve this? Why are you being so nice to me?" Infiniti just put her finger over Tier's lips so she would keep quiet.

"Just get some rest; you can pay me back later," and when Infiniti said that she meant it. She fixed Tier some soup, helped her use the bathroom, and kept a warm rag on her wounds. Inside her room she thought about what she was going to do to get back at the people that beat Tier up and what she was going to do to get back at Cardi, Mr. Punk Out.

Although, Tier left out the part that they were Goons which would explain the brutality of her beating and that the person that beat her up wasn't really a daily womanizer. Infiniti had her own problems to worry about, but that didn't matter being the type of woman she was.

-

Carmella stepped out her hotel room so that Cardi wouldn't hear her talking to Dakota happy that it was finally about to happen, it was finally about to go down, and Cardi was there.

"Hello?"

"Hi auntie I'm here."

"What took you so long?" Carmella asked knowing how long it took to get from Michigan to Illinois. I made a couple of detours, then I fell asleep at a rest stop, but I'm here."

"Okay I'm in Room 315 just come on up. The door will be open."

"Alright I'll see you in a minute. I'm probably going to swing by Bob Evans and grab me a bite."

"That'll be great," Carmella ended jumping up and down. Going back in the room, Carmella closed the door shut, but she didn't lock it. Carmella woke Cardi up with her kisses.

"You kissing me like you want to get something started," Cardi said waking up feeling Carmella's lips on him.

"That's because I do."

Since Cardi left Dakota, he didn't think about her not one time and was really considering the thought of being with Carmella since Dakota knew almost all of his dirt and Carmella didn't know any. Especially not since all he's been doing is seeing Carmella and pleasing her. As much as he claimed their little affair was wrong look how bad he was contradicting himself. Standing up Carmella slid off her lingerie so that she would be completely naked. And Cardi came out his boxers like it was hammertime. He liked to eat it up and then beat it up before he got to work so he got in between Carmella's legs and starting eating his breakfast and his brunch. She was glad they didn't get straight to doing it because she didn't want Dakota to miss the real Cardi even though she already knew who the man really was.

By the time Dakota was finished eating, Carmella and Cardi were still sexing and wasn't going to stop sexing anytime soon. In Carmella's head she was wishing that Dakota would hurry up.

Pulling into an empty parking space in the hotel parking lot, Dakota figured she'll just go straight upstairs and come back later to get her bag. Walking in the hotel she didn't know she was about to get into. There was no way to have known. She was expecting a stress-relieving vacation not a freak show. Soon as the elevator doors opened, Dakota walked in and pressed 3 before the elevator doors closed. She didn't even see Cardi's car in the parking lot, and she called herself not thinking about him either. Soon as Dakota got off the elevator she searched for Room 315 and wondered if she should knock, but she remembered her auntie said the door should be open so she walked in.

She heard noises and figured that her auntie was shacking up with some man she met at the hotel, but then she got closer. Close enough to see the man that her auntie had her legs wrapped around. Close enough to see the man that was on top of her auntie. Close enough to recognize that the man her auntie was shacking up with was Cardi.

"What the hell is this?" Dakota screamed and as she screamed tears came down her cheeks like her eyes were a running faucet. She screamed like people do on scary movies when they know somebody is screwing with them. Hearing Dakota's voice Cardi jumped back immediately and Carmella was completely satisfied even though she was putting herself in danger. Getting beat up by a girlfriend was the worst beating in the world, but Dakota didn't have any reason to fight.

"Out of all the females out here you had to cheat on me with my auntie and once again?" Cardi couldn't even speak and Carmella didn't peep the words that just exited Dakota's mouth. She was missing valuable information. There was nothing Cardi could say. Not sorry, not baby it's not what it looks like none of those methods or excuses would work.

"And Carmella you backstabbing bitch!" Dakota headed straight for her auntie so she could knock her out, but Cardi grabbed her as fast as he could predicting what she was probably about to do.

"I wouldn't do that if I was you unless you want to go to jail," Carmella warned sitting up.

"I want to go to jail so put me down Cardi! You don't have a right to touch me anymore! I don't ever want your dirty hands on me again!"

"Keep her away from me Cardi unless you want to kill our baby!" Both Cardi and Dakota froze.

"What?" Both Cardi and Dakota asked together.

"That's right boo I'm pregnant and I'm keeping it so I advise you to be a daddy or else I'm going straight to the Penobscot Building."

Hearing that Cardi dropped Dakota since he got caught with her elbow jabbing him straight in his rib cage.

"You two make me sick. I don't ever want to speak to either one of y'all again! Cardi were done so you can move in with your cougar now! And Carmella you can have his cheating ass and I quit your lame job! I'm done selling myself short for you're basic, hole in the wall, low class spot. I see why Luke divorced you was probably screwing his niece's boyfriend too! All this time y'all be sneaking behind my back to be bedroom-buddies, secret lovers, or whatever the hell y'all are, but I don't give a damn y'all can have each other!"

Carmella didn't care about what she had done to her niece. Dakota ran to her car and locked her doors. She put her key in the ignition, took some deep breathes, and sat in the parking lot. Back in the hotel Cardi and Carmella was wrapping that shit up.

"So when was you going to tell me you were pregnant and who said I'm ready to be a father?"

"I just told you and even if you ain't you better get ready. You got less than eight months to get your mind right! You should've used protection!"

"How in the hell is you goin set me up like that? This was supposed to be between me and you."

"Don't be embarrassed, y'all relationship wasn't going anywhere anyway. So here's your fresh start."

"That was some high school BS that you just pulled Carmella and I'm going outside to get some fresh air."

"I'm sorry that you feel that way, but I don't regret a thang." Cardi threw on a beater, some jeans, and some flip flops and walked outside to the parking lot. He saw Dakota's car after walking for a couple of minutes. He decided to say a word or two to her even though it wasn't anything he could say to her. Just as Cardi was walking up on her car, Dakota turned her key and put the car in reverse without looking back. She wasn't backing up slow either. By the time Cardi figured that Dakota was about to back up it was too late. Turning her wheel, Dakota took off for home. She didn't even hear the sound of her car hitting a body like she was deaf. She didn't look in any mirrors to check her blind spots or surroundings. She didn't even have the radio on. She was just gone in a whole another world speeding like Speedy Gonzales bound to get pulled over by the state boys. It was no way they were going to let her zoom past them without stopping her especially not on the highway.

She was definitely not going to make it home without going somewhere first. Speeding down the freeway the state boys started flashing their lights behind her after she got in about 10 minutes of reckless driving. Dakota didn't stop though she kept going, and before she knew it one police car turned into two. Two police cars turned into three, and three police cars turned into four all for one car, one driver, one girl who hadn't even committed a real crime because speeding wasn't a crime. It was a traffic violation, but fleeing from the police was. The police cars pulled on the side of Dakota, but she wouldn't budge. Lucky for the police Dakota's car fuel level was low. Forced to stop Dakota pulled over and rolled the windows down with the police right behind her. Dakota stepped out of the car on her own halfway, but she didn't close the door, or turn the car off. There was still a little bit of gas left, but it was no point of Dakota to keep going and risk being caught in the mist of traffic. She still had her foot on the brake which she held it there while she put the car in drive and hurried up and pulled her other foot to safety as her car went off by itself. The police couldn't believe what they were seeing. They had their guns drawn, and were on their way to cuff Dakota who had her hands in the air, crying, and walking towards the police.

Dakota's car didn't make it very far, but it was gone. It almost caused about five accidents, but other cars had enough space and sense to dodge the uncontrollable car that was trying to hit them. The police handcuffed Dakota like she was a convict that stole something or was trying to transport something, and she wanted to eliminate the evidence. She just played it off like she thought she put the car in park when indeed she had the car in park for a minute before the thought came to her to put the car in drive. She wasn't worried because she had people in high places and her little car stunt didn't injure anybody. At the most she was going to get a couple of days in the county, get a misdemeanor on her record, have to do some community service, probation, and/or anger management despite the list of charges that would be pending against her.

-

Cardi rolled over on the ground to his side then back to his back. His chest felt like it was going to collapse. Lifting up his shirt, he struggled to sit up, and took a look down at his stomach. He had a huge scar that covered mostly all of his stomach and his packs. Not to mention he had this kind of rainbow thing going on down there. His stomach was like five different colors and he looked bruised very badly. It took a lot out of him, but he finally got to his feet and headed for the room with Carmella. He touched anything and everything he could to help him walk using all the nearby objects as a crunch. He touched people's cars, trees, doors, walls, anything in arm's reach. Everybody that saw him struggling asked him was he okay and did he need anything, but he just ignored them and kept heading towards the room.

He slid his hotel key in the door and Carmella was thrilled to hear the door open. She was unsure if Cardi was still mad or not, but he couldn't be mad now not in his condition. Scooting to the bed Carmella could tell something was seriously wrong with Cardi.

"What happened baby?" Cardi just sat in the bed and Carmella shot up to her feet even though Cardi was already sitting on the bed trying to lay completely down.

"Dakota hit me with her car."

"Dakota did what? No! I'm about to go home and beat her ass!"

"No calm down I think she did it by accident. It's no telling where Dakota is going to be. Just leave it alone." There was no way in hell Carmella was just going to leave it alone. If anybody was going to be injuring her baby daddy it was going to be her. She was definitely going to cut her vacation short.

"Well do you need to go to the hospital or something? Is something broken?"

"I just want to sleep. I would tell you to put some ice on my stomach, but I don't think you want to see it so I'll take care of that when I wake up. Just don't get too close. Not saying you can't touch me or anything, but I'm kind of banged up right now." Carmella respected his wishes and as soon as he went to sleep she started pacing the floor brainstorming what the hell she was going to do to get back at Dakota.

TO BE CONTINUED